He turned and stared at Mariah's front door, wondering what he should do.

Why was he here? Why hadn't he gone home? He pushed himself forward and lightly tapped on the door. She opened it. Her soft curly hair spilled around her shoulders and her blue eyes radiated gentle concern as she looked at him. She wore the terry cloth robe she'd had on the night they made love. That night seemed as if it were a million years ago.

It was at that moment that Lucas realized he could fall in love with her, if he allowed it, and that there would be no happy ending. When this was all over, he feared that to her he would be just a bad memory.

And that she'd remember him as the man who broke her heart and never looked back.

CARLA CASSIDY

THE SHERIFF'S SECRETARY

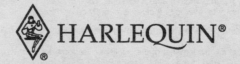

TORONTO • NEW YORK • LONDON
AMSTERDAM • PARIS • SYDNEY • HAMBURG
STOCKHOLM • ATHENS • TOKYO • MILAN • MADRID
PRAGUE • WARSAW • BUDAPEST • AUCKLAND

ISBN-13: 978-0-373-69344-3
ISBN-10:   0-373-69344-3

THE SHERIFF'S SECRETARY

www.eHarlequin.com

Printed in U.S.A.

ABOUT THE AUTHOR

Carla Cassidy is an award-winning author who has written more than fifty novels for Silhouette Books. In 1995, she won Best Silhouette Romance from *Romantic Times BOOKreviews* for her novel *Anything for Danny*. In 1998, she also won a Career Achievement Award for Best Innovative Series from *Romantic Times BOOKreviews*.

Carla believes the only thing better than curling up with a good book to read is sitting down at the computer with a good story to write. She's looking forward to writing many more books and bringing hours of pleasure to readers.

Books by Carla Cassidy

CAST OF CHARACTERS

Sheriff Lucas Jamison—He's desperate to find his missing sister and her young charge.

Mariah Harrington—Her entire world explodes when her son, Billy, disappears.

Jenny Jamison—Is Lucas's sister an innocent babysitter or part of a dangerous plot?

Frank Landers—Mariah's ex-husband had no interest in being a father, but would he kidnap his own son to torment the woman who left him?

Phil Ribideaux—Had the wealthy playboy—Jenny's ex-boyfriend—been driven to commit a crime when his father disinherited him?

Remy Troulous—The dangerous young man heads a gang called the Voodoo Priests. What was his connection with Jenny?

Louis DuBois, Wally Ellis and Ed Maylor—The sheriff's men were doing their best to solve the crime…weren't they?

Prologue

It had been easier than he'd expected. He drew a deep breath to calm the rush of adrenaline he'd sustained for the past hour and a half.

As the adrenaline eased, a new sense of euphoria flooded his veins. He'd done it. He'd actually managed to pull it off. All the months of planning had finally paid off.

To assure himself of his success, he walked across the shack's wooden floor and opened the slat in the door that offered him a view into the small room.

They were both still out, unconscious on the mat where he'd placed them when he'd carried them in from the boat. Billy had been easy. He probably weighed no more than fifty pounds.

Jenny had been more difficult. He'd struggled beneath her dead weight, not wanting to drop her into the gator-infested water that surrounded the shack.

They were out, but soon the drugs would wear off and they'd wake up and know they were trapped. They wouldn't know who had taken them or why they were here. And then the fear would begin.

Although, on the outside, the shack looked as if a stiff breeze could blow it over and into the murky waters of Conja Creek, that appearance was deceiving.

He'd spent the past month making sure the small interior room was strong and secure, like a fortress, not to keep people out but rather to keep people in. It was the perfect place for, when they woke, when they began to scream for help, there would be nobody to hear them but the gators and the fish.

He checked his watch, then closed the slat with a sigh of satisfaction. They had all the basic necessities they needed to survive until he returned here. But now it was time for him to go.

Minutes later he lowered himself into his boat. It would take him nearly an hour to maneuver through the maze of waterways half-choked with vegetation.

He didn't mind the time it would take. He'd use it to think about Sheriff Lucas Jamison, the golden boy who had it all. He tightened his hands on the boat's steering wheel. Sheriff Lucas Jamison, the confident know-it-all, the town's favorite son, the man who looked at him like he was nothing. Right now Lucas was the town's favorite son, but soon he would know what it was like to be terrified.

Chapter One

Mariah Harrington wasn't worried when she got home from work and found her eight-year-old son and her roommate missing. It was a gorgeous late-summer afternoon, and odds were good that Billy and Jenny had walked to the nearby park to enjoy an hour or so of outdoor fun. Jenny's car was in the driveway, so Mariah knew they couldn't have gone far.

She threw her keys on the kitchen table, stepped out of her navy high heels and opened the refrigerator to look for the can of soda that she'd hidden the night before in the vegetable bin. No chance Billy or Jenny would look in there. They both shared the same abhorrence for anything green and good for them.

Smiling as she carried the cold can into the living room, she thought of her son and her roommate. It was hard to believe how much an eight-year-old and a twenty-five-year-old could have in common. But in many ways Jenny was as much child as adult.

Of course, that came from being raised by an overly protective, domineering brother. Her smile fell away as she thought of Sheriff Lucas Jamison.

As the mayor's secretary, she often found herself acting as a buffer between the hardheaded Lucas and the ineffectual mayor of Conja Creek. But it wasn't her job that made her want to keep her distance from the handsome-as-sin sheriff.

There was a touch of judgment in his dark eyes and a command to his presence that made her think of dark days in her past—a past she'd finally managed to escape.

It had been Lucas who had approached her about renting a room to his younger sister. He'd thought Mariah would be a good influence on flighty, immature Jenny.

She popped the top of her soda and took a long swallow. She'd agreed to the idea of a roommate because financially it made sense and because the house was big enough that they could live together without being in each other's pockets.

Jenny had moved in two months ago. Mariah had found her to be charming but lacking in confidence, thanks to too much older brother and not enough life experience. It was an added benefit that Jenny and Billy had taken so well to each other. There were a lot of young women Jenny's age who wouldn't want to bother with an eight-year-old boy.

Mariah unfastened her hair from the neat ponytail at the nape of her neck and slithered her hands through the thick curls to massage her scalp. Then she leaned her head back against the sofa and released a deep, weary sigh.

It had been a long day. She was not only Mayor Richard Welch's secretary, she was also part therapist, errand runner and mommy to the man. Things were particularly hectic now with the mayoral election coming in less than three months. When Richard had won the election that had made him mayor, he'd run unopposed. This election he was facing two worthy opponents.

Checking her watch, she figured she had twenty minutes or so to sit and relax before she needed to make supper. Billy and Jenny would be back by six. They were never late for a meal.

She must have fallen asleep, for when she opened her eyes again the room held the semidarkness of late twilight. For a moment she was disoriented as to the day and time as she stared around the neat living room.

As sleep fell away, she remembered it was Friday night and she'd been waiting for Billy and Jenny to get home from the park. She checked her watch, the first faint alarm went off in her head. Almost seven. They should have been home an hour ago.

She pulled herself off the sofa and walked to the front door, trying to ignore the small niggle of worry that whispered in the back of her brain.

"They've been late once before," she whispered aloud, as if the audible sound of that thought could ease her concern. The last time, they'd found a stray dog caught in some brambles in the wooded area next to the park. It had taken them hours to calm the frightened mutt and get him untangled.

Mariah opened the door, stepped onto the front porch and looked in the direction of the park, hoping to see them hurrying toward the house with a tale of adventure to share. She saw nobody except Roger Olem, three doors down, watering his flowers.

In another half hour or so it would be full dark.

The humid evening air, redolent with the scent of flowers and sunshine, enveloped her as she left the porch and headed down the sidewalk in the direction of the park. As she made her way, she marveled at the happiness she'd found here.

She'd never meant to make Conja Creek, Louisiana, her home. It had simply been a blip on her road map when she'd left Shreveport on her way to anywhere.

It had taken only a single night spent at a local bed-and-breakfast to make her fall in love with the small, quaint bayou town.

She'd just about given up on happiness before landing here. Eight months ago, life had been about survival, but now she was a respected part of the community, and Billy was happier than she'd ever seen him.

She quickened her pace as the park came into view. If they were here, then she needed to have a talk with Jenny about making sure they got home on time when they decided to leave the house for a little fun.

Her heart dropped a bit when she saw that nobody sat on the swings or climbed on the jungle gym. The only person she saw in the park was one of her neighbors, Rosaline Graham who, since her husband's death, often spent the hours between dinner and bedtime sitting on a park bench.

"Hi, Rosaline," Mariah called to the old woman. "I don't suppose you've seen my son or Jenny Jamison lately, have you?"

She shook her head. "Sorry, honey. I just got here a few minutes ago, but I sure haven't seen them."

The alarm bells that had just been whispering

through Mariah's head suddenly pealed so loudly she could barely hear anything else.

Maybe they'd chosen another way home. Maybe they were there right now wondering where *she* was. She started back toward home. After several steps she broke into a run, telling herself not to panic. It wasn't as if it were the middle of the night. It was only about seven-thirty.

But when she got back to the house, there was still no sign of them. The phone had no messages, and the panic that had tried to take hold of her now grasped her with both hands.

She pulled out her address book and grabbed the phone. The reason Billy had been home today and not at his babysitter's was because he'd awakened with a sore throat. Maybe Jenny had taken him to the doctor's office.

The fact that Jenny's car was in the driveway didn't matter. From Mariah's house it was a short walk to Main Street, where Dr. Ralph Dell had his offices.

Her fingers shook as she punched in the phone number. Normally Mariah was the last to panic, and even though she thought there was surely a logical explanation for Billy and Jenny's absence, she couldn't help the swell of inexplicable fear that filled her chest.

By nine o'clock she had called everyone she knew to call. Friends, neighbors and schoolmates of Billy's. None of Billy's friends had seen him that day, nor had anyone seen Jenny.

She'd been reluctant to call Lucas, knowing that if Jenny and Billy came home and nothing was seriously wrong, Lucas would reprimand Jenny for the next week for worrying her.

But now she had no choice. With each minute that passed, the disquiet she'd felt since waking from her unexpected nap raged into full-blown fear.

She punched in the number for the sheriff's office, unsurprised when Lucas himself answered the call. "Sheriff Jamison." His deep, self-confident voice instantly commanded respect.

"Sheriff, it's Mariah Harrington. Have you by any chance seen Jenny or Billy today?"

"No. Why?" His voice held a sudden intensity and she could see him in her mind. The tight jaw, the disapproving line trekking across his forehead, the thin press of his lips.

"I'm sure there's a logical explanation, but I've been home since five-thirty and they aren't here." Although she tried to maintain her composure, her voice cracked and tears suddenly stung her eyes.

"I'll be right there." He didn't wait for her to reply.

Mariah hung up the receiver then walked back to the front door and stared outside, watching the night shadows as they moved in to steal the last of the day.

Fear clawed up the back of her throat as she realized that within fifteen minutes or so it would be night. Where was Jenny? And, dear God, where was her son?

LUCAS JAMISON climbed into his car and headed for the Harrington home, already forming the words to the lecture he'd deliver to his sister when he saw her.

God bless that girl, he thought. Sometimes she just didn't use the brains that she'd been born with. She'd probably taken Billy for ice cream, or decided to get him a burger at the café and had neglected to leave a note.

He just hoped this little escapade didn't screw up the living arrangement with Mariah. When Jenny's last boyfriend had broken up with her, she'd not only lost the man she'd believed was the love of her life but also her living space. She'd refused to move back to the family home with Lucas and had bunked on a girlfriend's sofa for a couple of weeks.

It had been Lucas who approached Mariah about Jenny renting a room from her. He knew Mariah was a widow, alone with her son, and lived in a big enough house that a renter might not be a problem.

But that wasn't the real reason he'd approached the mayor's secretary.

Despite being only twenty-nine years old, Mariah carried herself like a much older, much more mature woman. No-nonsense and with cold blue eyes that could freeze a man in his path, she could potentially have the steadying effect on Jenny that Lucas had never managed. Or so he hoped.

"Jenny, what have you done this time?" he muttered as he pulled up to the curb in front of the Harrington house. He hadn't even turned off the engine before Mariah flew out of the house.

Her chestnut hair, normally pulled back in a tight ponytail, sprung in wild curls around her petite features, making her look far younger than she appeared when she was at her desk in the mayor's office.

He didn't have to ask if Jenny and Billy had shown up. The answer to the unspoken question shone from Mariah's worried blue eyes.

"I'm glad you're here," she said, her usually cool, composed voice holding a telltale tremble.

"I'm sure there's nothing to worry about," he said as he fell into step with her and headed back toward the house. "If I know my sister, this is all just some crazy misunderstanding, and she and Billy are probably down at the café eating pie or star-watching down at the park."

"I've been to the park. They weren't there." She opened the front door and ushered him into the small entryway. When she turned to face him, her eyes flashed with a touch of impatience. "And I haven't known your sister as long as you have, but I know her well enough to know that she wouldn't just take off with Billy and not let me know where they are. Something's wrong. Something is terribly wrong."

She might think she knew Jenny, but Jenny had obviously been on her best behavior since moving in here. "You mind if I look around?" Lucas asked. In the two months that Jenny had lived here he'd only been as far as the front porch. Jenny had insisted that this was her space and she didn't want him checking up on her. He tightened his jaw. Obviously *somebody* needed to check up on her.

"Please, be my guest," Mariah said. "I've already looked in Jenny's room to see if she might have left a note for me there, but I didn't find one."

"Which room is hers?"

She gestured down the hallway. "Second door on the right."

She didn't follow him, but instead moved back to the front door as if she could make them appear on the doorstep by sheer willpower alone.

Mariah's house was exactly what he'd imagined it would be—slightly old-fashioned and immaculately clean. As he grabbed the doorknob to Jenny's room he steeled himself for the chaos inside.

He adored his baby sister, but Jenny had always seemed most comfortable in the middle of chaos and drama. He hoped like hell she hadn't orchestrated this to get attention. It was one thing to be a drama queen in your own life. It was quite another to involve an eight-year-old boy.

Her room was actually fairly neat, except the bed hadn't been made and a pair of jeans had been thrown across a chair in the corner. He looked on the nightstand, checked the small desk but found no note, no clue as to where she might have gone with a little boy in tow.

Billy's room was next door. Bunk beds stood against one wall, the lower bunk not made. A small toy box sat beneath a window. Lucas walked to the window and checked it out. The screen was in place and nothing seemed to be amiss.

The third bedroom had to be Mariah's. He opened the door and paused in surprise at the sight of the king-size bed covered with a scarlet spread and plump matching pillows. Fat candles stood on the nightstand, their dark wicks letting him know they weren't just for decoration but were burned regularly.

So, the cool and distant Ms. Harrington had a sensual side. Lucas was surprised by the little burst of heat that filled his stomach at the thought of her in the bed, candlelight stroking her features.

He frowned and shut the door behind him. He flipped open his cell phone and called his office.

"Deputy Ellis," a deep voice boomed.

"Hey, Wally, it's me," Lucas said.

"Hi, boss, what's up?"

"I want you to get a couple of the guys and check out the café, the bowling alley, the movie theater, places like that. I'm looking for my sister."

"Problems?"

Lucas hesitated. "Jenny's late getting back to the Harrington house and we don't know where she is. I wouldn't be so worried, but she's got Mariah's little boy with her."

"Sure, no problem. I'll call you back when we find them."

Lucas tucked his cell phone back into his pocket, then walked back down the hallway.

He found Mariah where he'd left her, standing sentry at the front door. She didn't hear his approach, and he paused at the end of the hallway to study her.

Though she'd been in town for almost a year, he knew almost nothing about her. He'd heard through the grapevine that she was a widow, and he knew she was a formidable barrier he often had to bulldoze through to speak with the dolt who called himself mayor. But he had no idea where she'd come from before she'd landed in Conja Creek.

As he watched, she tapped two slender fingers against the glass door, as if sending an SOS message in Morse code. Standing at the door, peering out into the deepening night, she looked smaller, more fragile than he could have imagined.

A protectiveness surged inside him and he reached out and touched her shoulder. She jumped and whirled around, as if she'd forgotten he was there. "Sorry, I didn't mean to startle you," he said.

"No, I just…" Her eyes darkened to a midnight blue. "Where could they be?"

"Why don't we go into the kitchen. Maybe you could make some coffee while we wait."

"Wait? Shouldn't you be rallying the troops? Getting together a search party?" Her chin rose a notch even as a sheen of tears misted her eyes. "You expect me to just sit and drink coffee while my son is someplace out there in the dark?"

"I've already rallied the troops. I've got my men looking now and yeah, there's nothing much to do but have some coffee and wait." He swallowed a sigh. "Look, Mariah, right now all we know is that Billy and Jenny are late getting home. There's no evidence that a crime occurred, no indication that this is anything more than my sister's thoughtlessness. Maybe she took Billy to a movie and lost track of time. I'm sure she's going to waltz in here before long, and she'll be shocked that you were so worried. Now, how about that coffee?"

She held his gaze for a long moment, then nodded and headed for the kitchen. As she began the coffee preparations Lucas sat at the oak table.

"I thought Billy went to a babysitter on the days you worked in the summer," he said.

"Normally he does, but he woke up this morning with a sore throat. Jenny offered to stay home with him."

"I thought she had those job interviews today." Lucas frowned. He'd been the one to set up the two interviews for his sister for that afternoon.

"She called yesterday and canceled. She didn't feel

like either job was what she was looking for," Mariah explained.

Lucas tamped down an edge of familiar frustration. "Did you speak to Jenny at all today?"

As the coffee began to drip into the carafe Mariah walked over to the table but didn't sit. "I spoke to her around ten this morning." Nervous energy rolled off her as her gaze shot to the kitchen window.

"Did she mention any plans for tonight?"

She focused her gaze back on him, and he saw a desperate fear screaming from the depths of her eyes. "No…nothing. Please, you need to do something. Jenny wouldn't do this to me. Something is wrong."

Lucas looked at his watch. Almost ten-thirty. He hadn't realized how late it had become. For the first time since he'd gotten the call from Mariah, a whisper of deep concern swept through him.

Sure, Jenny had pulled some stunts in the past that had made him want to wring her neck, but he couldn't imagine her pulling this kind of disappearing act with eight-year-old Billy in tow.

She turned back to the counter to pour them each a cup of coffee, but Lucas was suddenly in no mood to sit idle. The fact that his phone remained silent indicated that none of his deputies had run across them. Conja Creek was a small town, and it shouldn't take this long for his men to find her…if she was someplace where she could be found.

He drew a breath of relief as his cell phone rang. He grabbed it from his shirt pocket and flipped it open. "Sheriff Jamison," he said. There was a moment of silence. "Hello?"

"Twinkle twinkle little star, only I know where they are. A game of hide-and-seek we'll play. Let's see if you can save the day." The voice was deep, guttural and sent shock waves through Lucas. Before he could reply, the caller clicked off.

Chapter Two

Mariah saw the blood leave Lucas's face as he checked the caller ID box, then slowly closed his phone and placed it on the table. Rich, raw fear invaded her, chilling her to the bone. She sank into the chair opposite him, afraid her legs would no longer hold her up.

"Did they find them?" Her head pounded with nauseating tension. "Please, tell me. Is he...are they..." She couldn't say the word.

"No! No, that wasn't one of my deputies," Lucas said hurriedly. A muscle ticked in his taut jaw, and for the first time since he'd arrived, she saw a touch of something deep and dark in his eyes. That frightened her as much as anything.

"Then who was on the phone?" She didn't want to know, was afraid of what he was going to tell her, and yet she *had* to know. She drew a steadying breath.

"I don't know who was on the phone. The call shows up as private on the ID. The caller indicated that he has Jenny and Billy and that a game of hide-and-seek has commenced."

She stared at him for a moment, unable to make

sense of his words. Hide-and-seek? That was one of Billy's favorite games. But this wasn't a game. This was something awful. As she tried to absorb what he'd just told her, he called the sheriff's office.

"Wally," he said into his phone. "Get all the men together and meet me at Mariah Harrington's house. We have a situation here."

A situation. Is that what this was? She swallowed against the scream that threatened to rip its way out of her throat. Billy. Where was Billy and who had taken him?

Calm. Stay calm, she told herself. It wouldn't do any good to fall to pieces. She had to stay calm and focused for whatever came next.

"What happens now?" She was surprised by the composure of her voice when inside she was quietly shattering apart.

He rose from the table. "I'll take a closer look around. We can talk to neighbors and see if anyone saw anything here today." His dark eyes gave away nothing of his thoughts.

Did he feel the same panic for his sister as she felt for her son? Oh, God. As the full impact sank in, she began to tremble. "What can I do? Shouldn't I be out asking questions? Looking for him?"

Lucas placed a hand on her shoulder as if to steady her rising hysteria, then returned to his chair in front of her. "Can you tell me if Jenny was seeing anyone in particular?"

She frowned and tried to focus on his question. "You mean dating?" She shook her head. "She was still nursing her wounds from when Phil Ribideaux broke up with her a couple of months ago." She twisted her fingers in her lap. "But, I don't know what she did or who she saw while I was at work every day. Do you think somebody she was seeing might be behind this?"

"I'm not sure what to think at this point." He got up once again. "I'm going to go check around again. We'll find them, Mariah. Try not to worry. We'll find them."

He left her there, and she knew he was going back to Jenny's room. Try not to worry? Was the man insane? She got up from the chair, unable to sit still another minute longer.

Why on earth would somebody want to kidnap Billy? As her mind whirled with suppositions, she realized she didn't want to go there. Too many of the answers were too terrifying.

A sob choked up from the depths of her as she moved to the window and peered outside into the black of night. Billy didn't like the dark. Now he was out there somewhere, being held by someone so he couldn't come home.

Cold. She'd never felt so cold. She squeezed her eyes shut and willed herself to remember every moment of that morning. She'd been in a hurry. She'd overslept and had rushed around to get ready for work.

When she'd awakened Billy, and he'd complained of a sore throat, she'd barely taken time to console him. She'd taken his temperature, which had been normal, had given him a brisk pat on the head, then had left for work knowing Jenny would handle things for the day.

All she wanted to do now was turn back the hands on the clock, somehow retrieve the precious morning. This time, when Billy complained of a sore throat, she would call in to work and take the day off. She'd stay home with her son and make him chicken noodle soup for lunch and peanut butter sandwiches with the crust cut off just the way he liked them.

She'd stay home, and he'd be safe. Another sob escaped her and she pressed her fingers against her lips in an attempt to suppress it.

She turned away from the window and headed to his bedroom. As she entered, the first thing that caught her eye was the inhaler on the nightstand, along with the nebulizer that had gotten Billy through a rough attack on many nights.

She whirled out of the bedroom and bumped into Lucas coming out of Jenny's room. "Lucas, Billy has asthma and they didn't take his inhaler. If he gets stressed or scared he'll have an attack and…" Her voice trailed off, the sentence too horrifying to finish.

"Mariah, what I need from you is a recent photo of Billy." His voice was calm, as if he hadn't heard what she'd just told him.

"Billy has asthma," she repeated.

"I heard you." His dark eyes held her gaze intently. "But we can't do anything about that right now. We have to stay focused on the things we can do. Now, I need a picture of Billy."

Somehow his words penetrated through the veil of despair that threatened to consume her. She nodded, grateful for something, anything to do.

She went to the desk in the living room and grabbed the framed photo that sat on top. It was the school portrait taken last year. She stared at it. Until this moment she hadn't realized how much he'd changed in the past several months. His dark hair was longer than it had been when the photo was taken, and his face was thinner. He'd been missing a front tooth then. Imagining his beautiful little face in her mind once again brought the press of tears to her eyes.

She set the photo back on the desk and began to dig through the top drawer. It suddenly seemed important that she find the perfect picture of her son.

In a frenzy she searched, more frantic with each second that passed. Her fingers finally landed on an envelope of photos she'd recently had developed. She opened the envelope and pulled out the photos.

The most recent one she had of Billy was of him and Jenny together. She picked it up and traced a finger over Billy's dark, unruly hair. His smile was filled with mischief as he grinned into the camera while making horns with his fingers behind Jenny's head.

Jenny's pretty face smiled back at Mariah from the photo, and her heart squeezed tighter. In the two months that Jenny had been living with her, Mariah had come to care about the younger woman a great deal.

"Did you find one?" Lucas came to stand behind her. She could smell his scent, a subtle cologne she always noticed when he came in to see the mayor. Funny how the familiar scent calmed her just a bit. She turned to face him with the picture in her hand.

"You can use this one. It's of Billy and Jenny together."

He took it from her, and she watched him study it. Other than a muscle knotting in his jaw, there was no sign of emotion. Before he could say anything, the doorbell rang and the deputies began to arrive.

A total of five deputies took their orders from Lucas.

They all gathered in the living room. Mariah sat on the sofa, numbed by the events swirling around her as Lucas took control.

"Wally, you and Ben start canvassing the neighborhood, see if anyone saw anything here today," Lucas said. "John, we need recording equipment placed on Mariah's phone in case a ransom call comes in."

Mariah sat up straighter. "Ransom?" Her gaze shot around to each of the men in the room. "But, I don't have any money to speak of."

"If this is about a ransom, I reckon the kidnapper figures Lucas can pay big bucks to get his sister back safe and sound," Deputy Ed Maylor said.

Lucas's jaw once again tightened in his lean face. "Let's just hope if this *is* about a ransom, we get a call soon." He looked at Deputy Louis DuBois. "Louis, I need you to see if you can get into Jenny's e-mail, find out if there's anything weird there. I tried to log on earlier, but she has it password protected."

The tall, thin man nodded. "It shouldn't take me too long to find a way around the protection."

"And what about me?" Deputy Maylor asked.

"Check all the windows and doors, see if you find any evidence of tampering," Lucas replied.

As the men all left to begin their jobs, Lucas joined Mariah on the sofa. To her surprise, he took one of her hands in his and gently squeezed. The warmth of his big hands around her ice-cold fingers felt good. "You doing okay?" he asked.

"No. I want to scream. I want to claw somebody's eyes out." She wanted somebody to hold her, somebody to tell her that everything was going to be fine, that Billy would be back in her arms in a matter of minutes. But Mariah had never had anyone to hold her when she was afraid, to calm her when she was upset.

She released Lucas's hands as she suddenly realized she was going to have to tell Lucas the truth about herself, about her past. She was going to have to confess that her life here in Conja Creek was built on lies.

It was possible Frank had found them, and it was equally possible he'd taken Billy. Jenny could have just been at the wrong place at the wrong time. And even though she knew that telling Lucas would destroy the facade of respectability she'd worked so hard to create, she'd do whatever it took to get Billy back.

"I have to tell you something," she said. "I don't know of anyone Jenny was seeing who might be involved in this, but I know somebody from my past who might be."

Lucas sat up straighter. "Who?"

Mariah clasped her hands together. Even thinking about the man whose name she was about to utter created a knot of new fear in her chest. "His name is Frank Landers, and last I knew he lived in Shreveport."

A deep frown etched across Lucas's forehead as he pulled a notepad and pen from his pocket. "What's his relationship to you and why would he want to kidnap Billy?"

She drew a deep breath. "He's my ex-husband and Billy's father."

LUCAS LOOKED AT HER in surprise. Her ex-husband? "I thought you were a widow, that Billy's father was dead."

Her blue eyes refused to meet his as she stared at her hands in her lap. "That's because I wanted everyone to believe I was a widow. Because I wanted to forget Frank Landers and my marriage to him."

"You need to unforget now," he said with an edge of impatience.

She reached up and twisted a strand of her hair between two fingers. "Frank and I were married for five years. We've been divorced for two. We lived in Shreveport." She dropped her hand to her lap and rubbed her left wrist like an arthritis sufferer feeling a weather front moving in.

"If you've been divorced for two years, why would your ex-husband decide to grab Billy now?" Lucas asked.

She looked at Lucas. Her cool blue eyes betrayed nothing of what might be going on inside her head. "I don't know. It's possible it took him all this time to locate us."

"He didn't know where you and Billy were going when you left Shreveport?"

She shook her head. "*I* didn't know where we were going when we left Shreveport, and I haven't been in touch with Frank since before my divorce."

He was less interested in what she was saying and more intrigued by what she wasn't telling him. "You don't have a custody arrangement with him?" he asked.

"I have full custody."

He waited for her to elaborate, but she didn't. The woman definitely had secrets, but he didn't have time to be curious about her past.

All he cared about was finding Jenny and Billy, and if she thought this Frank Landers might be responsible, then he needed to call the Shreveport police and see if they could locate the man.

"You have an address for him?" he asked.

"I imagine he still lives in our old house." She told him the address and he wrote it down.

"I'll contact the Shreveport police and see if they can hunt him down." Lucas looked at his watch. Almost midnight. Hopefully the authorities in Shreveport could go to Frank's home and find out if he was there. It was a five-hour drive from Conja Creek to Shreveport. Even if Frank was home, he could have taken Billy and Jenny and gotten back by now.

He tried not to think about where Jenny might be. If Frank Landers had come to get his kid, then what had he done with Jenny?

Mariah stood, her entire body taut with tension and her eyes haunted. "If he's taken Billy it isn't because he wants his son. It's because he wants to hurt me."

He'd always looked at Mariah as nothing more than a barrier he needed to get through to see the mayor, a respectable widow who might be a good influence on his flighty, dramatic sister. Now he saw her as neither of those things, but rather as a woman who had apparently suffered some sort of heartache in her past. Lucas knew all about heartache.

"Within an hour we should know if Frank is in Shreveport. In the meantime, why don't you make a fresh pot of coffee? My deputies should be checking in anytime and they'd probably appreciate the caffeine since it's getting so late."

He knew the moment those last words left his mouth that they were the wrong thing to say. She lifted her wrist to check her watch, and her features seemed to crumble into themselves as a sheen of tears filled her eyes.

"Billy has never been away from me this long," she said, but before he could reply she left the living room and disappeared into the kitchen.

The next couple of hours passed in agonizingly slow increments. Lucas called the state police, and an Amber Alert went out. He also spoke to the FBI, who indicated they would have a field agent there the next morning. The deputies checked in with the news that nobody had seen anything suspicious at the home during the day.

"I'm not surprised," Mariah said. "All my neighbors work except Sarah Gidrow across the street, and she spends most of her days watching soap operas in the family room in the back of the house."

They couldn't be sure Mariah's house was a crime scene, which was problematic. There was no sign of a struggle, nothing to indicate that anything untold had happened there. It was possible the crime scene was the front yard, or the park, or a sidewalk a block away.

Jenny's e-mail had yielded nothing to raise an eyebrow, and Deputy Maylor had reported that there was no sign of forced entry or tampering at any of the windows or doors, leaving Lucas to suspect that if the crime *had* happened here, Jenny had opened the door to whomever had taken them.

If they'd really been taken.

It was that particular thought that haunted him as the night hours passed. Were Jenny and Billy really in danger from a kidnapper, or had Jenny orchestrated this whole drama? What better way to get the attention of Phillip Ribideaux, the young man who had recently broken her heart?

Although this was certainly beyond the pale of any stunt Jenny had pulled in the past, he had to admit that it was something he thought she might be capable of doing.

It was in her genes. He had plenty of memories of his mother pulling crazy stunts in an effort to hang on to whatever man happened to be in her life at the time.

He shoved away those thoughts, not wanting to remember the woman who had possessed the maternal instincts of a rock. She'd died when Jenny was twelve and Lucas was twenty-two, and for the past thirteen years Lucas had spent his time raising Jenny and trying to make sure she didn't turn out like Elizabeth, their mother.

Despite the late hour, he began calling Jenny's friends to find out if anyone had spoken to her that day or knew where she might have gone.

Mariah sat on the edge of the sofa and listened to him making those calls. With each minute that passed, the tension that rolled off her increased and her eyes gazed at him with the silent demand that he do something, anything, to bring her baby boy back home.

By three he had nobody else to call, nothing else to do but wait until morning or for another phone call to come in.

"You still aren't sure that they've been taken by somebody, are you?" she asked when he hung up the phone after talking to one of Jenny's girlfriends. There was a touch of censure in Mariah's eyes.

"I have to look at all possibilities," he replied non-committally.

"It must be terrible, to always look for the worst in the people around you."

He eyed her in surprise. There was an edge in her voice that made him wonder if she was trying to pick a fight. He stared at her assessingly.

Even though exhaustion showed in the shadows beneath her eyes and her forehead was lined with worry, somehow she looked lovely. He'd never really noticed before how pretty she was. But she also looked achingly fragile, as if the mighty control she'd exhibited over the past hours might snap at any moment.

"I'm just doing my job," he said, refusing to be drawn into an argument with the mother of a missing eight-year-old. "Why don't you try to get some sleep?" he suggested. "We've done everything we can do for now."

She sighed and swept a hand through her cascade of chestnut curls. "So, we just wait." Her voice was flat, without inflection. It wasn't a question, but rather a statement.

Lucas didn't reply. He knew there was nothing he could say that would make things better for her. There was no way he could tell her that, no matter what happened, he didn't see a happy ending.

If Jenny were responsible for this, then he would have to do his duty and arrest her for kidnapping. If Frank Landers had taken Billy, then what had he done with Jenny? The answers that sprang to his mind chilled his blood. And if somebody had taken Jenny for ransom, then Billy was expendable.

No matter what, Lucas had the terrible feeling that a tragedy lay ahead and there was nothing he could do to stop it from happening.

THE FIRST THING Jenny became aware of was a headache the likes of which she'd never had before. She winced and reached up to grab the back of her pounding head. Slowly, other sensations and impressions began to seep through her mind.

The smell of rotting fish and dampness coupled with the faint sound of water lapping against wood. The sound of insects buzzing and clicking. She opened her eyes and was terrified when she saw nothing but blackness.

Where am I? The question screamed through her head, making it pound with more nauseating intensity. Panic surged inside her as she sat up, fighting back a scream of sheer terror.

Before she could release the scream, a faint whimper sounded from someplace beside her. And with that whimper, memory returned.

She and Billy had been sitting on the sofa watching cartoons. Billy had gotten up to the bathroom…and somebody had come into the house.

One minute she'd been laughing at the antics of the Road Runner, and the next her mouth and nose had been covered with something that must have rendered her almost immediately unconscious.

"Billy?" She tentatively moved a hand and encountered his warm little body next to her.

"Jenny?" He scooted closer to her as another whimper escaped him.

"Are you okay, buddy?" She pulled him against her and wrapped him in her arms. "Are you hurt?"

"My head hurts and I want my mommy."

"I know, honey. But you're going to have to be brave for a little while, okay?"

She felt him nod. "Where is this place?" he asked. "Why did that man bring us here?" Billy's body trembled slightly against her and she thought she detected a faint wheeze in his voice.

With each minute that passed, Jenny's mind grew clearer. "Did you see the man, Billy? Did you see what he looked like?" If she knew who had done this, then maybe she could figure out why.

"He had on a black mask. I tried to run, but then he grabbed me and put something over my face and I guess I went to sleep."

A man with a mask. What was going on? Who had drugged them and brought them here...wherever here was? Once again a scream of terror rose up inside her, but she swallowed against it, knowing that she had to maintain control. She needed to be brave, not for herself but for Billy. If she lost it, that would only frighten Billy more than he already was.

"Somebody took us, Jenny, and I'll bet my mom doesn't know where I am." The wheeze in Billy's voice wasn't just a figment of her imagination.

"Don't be scared, Billy." She reached her hand up to touch his sweaty head, then rubbed the back of her hand against his damp cheek. "Even if your mom doesn't know where we are, my brother will help her find us. You know Lucas is the sheriff. He's very smart and he'll find us in no time." She hoped he believed her.

She certainly wanted to believe her own words. Billy seemed to relax a bit.

"I think it's the middle of the night. Maybe we should both go back to sleep, then we can figure out how to get home in the morning," she said. There was nothing that could be done in the utter darkness that surrounded them.

"Okay." Billy cuddled closer to her and she could tell by his breathing that he went back to sleep almost immediately.

Sleep was the last thing on Jenny's mind as she fought against a fear the likes of which she'd never known. She had no idea what kind of place they were in, was afraid to explore in the blackness that prevailed. She had no idea who had taken them and why.

There was only one thing she was fairly certain of and it didn't take a rocket scientist to realize it. The buzz of insects, the smell of fish and the sound of water all led her to believe they were someplace deep in the swamp.

As she thought of all the miles of waterways, the hundreds of miles of tangled, dangerous swampland that surrounded Conja Creek, a new despair gripped her, and she prayed that her brother would be able to find them before it was too late.

Chapter Three

Lucas pulled into his driveway at six the next morning. His intention was to take a fast shower, then go talk to Phillip Ribideaux to see if the young man had any clue as to where Jenny and Billy might be.

When he'd left Mariah's house, she'd been seated in the same chair where she'd sat for most of the night, staring out the window as dawn slowly arrived. He'd left her in the charge of Deputy Ed Maylor, who would hold down the fort there while Lucas did a little field investigation. Maylor was a good man, bright and eager to get ahead.

The Jamison home was a huge two-story antebellum mansion that sat on five acres of lush lawn. Lucas's father had been sixty when he married his young bride, Elizabeth. He'd made a fortune playing the stock market with his old family money. He'd died when Lucas was eleven and Jenny was just a baby.

Lucas didn't have many father-son memories. His father had spent most of his time either in his office at home or in bed with a heart condition that had eventually killed him. Although Lucas would always believe it had been his mother's demands and histrionics that had killed his old man.

"Have you found them?" Marquette Dupre met him at the door, her black eyes radiating with worry.

"No, I'm just here to take a quick shower then go have a chat with Phillip Ribideaux," Lucas said as he headed for the grand staircase. Marquette followed close at his heels as he headed up to his bedroom suite.

"That boy needs less money and more character, that's for sure," Marquette exclaimed. "You think he knows where Jenny and that little boy is?"

"I don't know." He stopped at the top of the stairs and turned to face the woman who had been the house-keeper for first his parents and now him. "Jenny hasn't said anything to you that I should know about, has she?"

Marquette's tiny face wreathed into something that looked like a prune. "You know better than that. That girl quit confiding in me when she was sixteen and I told you that she sneaked out of the house to meet that boy she had a crush on. How's Mariah doing?"

Lucas walked into his bedroom and sat on the edge of the bed to take off his boots. "I'm not sure how, but she's managing to hold it together."

"That don't surprise me. That's one strong woman. You can see it in her eyes. She's got that cold gator stare. Besides, she'd have to be a strong woman to put up with that boob we elected mayor of this fine city."

Lucas offered her a grim smile, then disappeared into the bathroom. Minutes later, standing beneath a hot spray of water, he did what he'd done through most of the nighttime hours: In his head, over and over again, he replayed the phone message he'd received.

There had been something familiar…not about the voice, which had obviously been disguised, but in the inflection, in the cadence of the words spoken. A kidnapper, or a friend of his sister's working with her to orchestrate drama?

He'd heard from the authorities in Shreveport, who had let him know that Frank Landers no longer lived at the address Mariah had given him. They promised to continue to look for him. He'd called Mariah with the news and she'd been bitterly disappointed that Frank hadn't been found.

Aware of minutes ticking off, he finished his shower and left the bathroom to see a clean, freshly pressed uniform laid out on his bed. Marquette was as handy as a pocket in a shirt.

Minutes later, dressed and with a thermos of fresh coffee, courtesy of his housekeeper, he drove toward Phillip Ribideaux's place. The shower had invigorated him, washing away the exhaustion that had weighed him down as he'd driven from Mariah's house to his own.

He hoped that, while he was hunting down leads this morning, Mariah was getting some much-needed sleep. There was nothing she could do at the moment to help bring her son home, and being exhausted would only make things worse.

He thought of what Marquette had said about Mariah. He'd known she was a strong woman, but through the long hours of the night he'd seen flashes of intense vulnerability. If she had an Achilles' heel it was definitely her son.

His hands tightened on the steering wheel as her

strange words to him echoed in his head. *It must be terrible, to always look for the worst in the people around you.* He had the distinct feeling she'd been talking about his relationship with his sister.

But she didn't really know Jenny. She didn't know the fear Lucas lived with every day—the fear that his sister would turn into another version of their mother and come to the same kind of tragic end.

Phillip Ribideaux lived in a large, attractive house on the outskirts of town. The twenty-eight-year-old had never worked a day in his life and lived off the generosity of his father, a wealthy developer in the area.

He was a party guy with no work ethic and a sense of privilege that Lucas had seen too often in men who came from money. In fact, Lucas himself and four of his then closest friends might have come to the same end had they not made a pact in college to use their wealth to give back to the community.

Lucas hadn't been sad to see the relationship between Ribideaux and Jenny end. Jenny deserved better than a man like Ribideaux.

It was just after seven when Lucas knocked on Ribideaux's front door. Phillip's sleek sports car was parked out front, but the knock yielded no reply. He rapped again, harder and longer this time.

"All right, all right." The deep male voice was full of irritation. Phil opened the door and glared at Lucas. It was obvious he'd been awakened by the knocking. His dark hair was mussed, a pillow crease indented his cheek and he wore only a pair of black silk boxers.

"Morning, Phil," Lucas said. "Can I come in?"

The handsome young man frowned. "Why? What's going on?" He scratched the center of his chest, then stifled a yawn with the back of his hand.

"I need to talk to you."

"Couldn't it wait? Jeez, what time is it?"

"No, it can't wait," Lucas replied.

"Talk about what?" He gazed at Lucas belligerently.

"I'd like to come in. Now, you can invite me inside and we can have a nice, friendly chat or I can come back in a little while with a search warrant and the chat won't be quite so friendly." Lucas kept his voice pleasant and calm, but narrowed his eyes to let Phil know he was dead serious.

With reluctance Phil opened the door to allow Lucas to enter. "Now you want to tell me what's going on?" he asked.

Lucas ignored the question and walked through the foyer and into the living room. He stopped in surprise, noting the moving boxes lining the walls and the lack of furniture. He turned back to face Phil. "Going someplace?"

"I'm moving, not that it's any business of yours," Phil replied.

"Where to?"

"To an apartment in town. Dad sold this place." A flash of anger shone from the young man's eyes. It was there only a moment, then gone. "Look, Sheriff, you want to tell me what this is about? I've got a lot of things to do today and I'm not in the mood for you."

Lucas tamped down a touch of rising anger. "When was the last time you spoke to Jenny?"

Phil visibly relaxed. "Is that what this is about? Your

sister? Whatever she told you, it's probably a lie. I haven't seen or talked to her for a couple of weeks."

"So you don't know anything about her disappearance?"

"Disappearance? Is she missing?"

"Yeah, since last night." Lucas studied Phil's features carefully, but it was impossible for him to discern if the man was lying or not. "So, you haven't seen or heard from her in the last couple of days?"

"Look, your sister's a nice girl and all that, but she was way too intense for me. We'd only been dating a couple of months and she starts talking about marriage and having kids and the whole traditional route. There's no way I'm ready for that, especially right now with everything such a mess."

"Everything such a mess?"

Phil averted his gaze from Lucas. "Private stuff. It has nothing to do with Jenny. I haven't had anything to do with Jenny for weeks, so if we're through here, I've got things to do." His gaze still didn't meet Lucas's.

Without a search warrant, there was little else Lucas could do here, and no judge in his right mind would give Lucas a warrant to search these premises on Lucas's hunch that Phil was hiding something.

"Where exactly is the new apartment?" Lucas asked as Phil walked him back to the front door.

"The Lakeside Apartments for the time being. Apartment 211." Phil grinned, the boyish, charming smile that had managed to get him into the beds of half the young women of Conja Creek. "I'm anxious to get out of this place. Owning a house is way too much responsibility for me."

Minutes later, as Lucas drove back to Mariah's place, he made mental notes to himself. It was obvious that Phil Ribideaux's life was in flux at the moment. Could that have anything to do with Jenny and Billy's disappearance?

Phil had seemed genuinely surprised to hear that Jenny was missing, but he was a smooth operator and Lucas knew the kid could lie without blinking an eye. And he'd definitely been hiding something. Something private, he'd said.

Tension twisted Lucas's gut as he drove. It had been almost twenty-four hours since anyone had spoken to Jenny and Billy, and there wasn't a lead in sight... except for a haunting voice on his cell phone that had promised a game of hide-and-seek.

"Jenny, if you've done something stupid, then please have the courage to undo it now," he murmured aloud. He hated suspecting that his sister had somehow orchestrated all this, but the alternative was far more terrifying.

He pulled his cell phone from his pocket and called Wally, his right-hand man. "Wally, I want you to do a little investigation into Phil Ribideaux. Find out from his friends what's going on in his life, and I want a tail put on him. Get Louis to do it. I want to know everyplace he goes and everyone he talks to."

"Got it," Wally replied. "Anything else?"

"Nothing for now." Lucas clicked off. He had no idea if Ribideaux had anything to do with this, but he definitely knew something was out of whack in the man's life.

As he turned the corner that led to Mariah's house he sucked in a breath. The place looked like a circus.

Cars were parked up and down the street, and the local news crew truck was parked in her yard. Mariah definitely hadn't been sleeping while he'd been gone.

Mayor Richard Welch stood in front of a camera with a reporter, his chest puffed up with self-importance. The man never missed a chance to get his mug in front of the voters.

Unwilling to be part of the mayor's photo op, Lucas skirted the house to the back door. Ed Maylor met him as he walked inside. "I told her you wouldn't like this, but she wouldn't listen to me," he said.

Lucas clapped the young deputy on the back. "It's all right. Why don't you go home, get some sleep. I'll take care of things here."

Maylor nodded and left by the back door. As he walked out, Sawyer Bennett entered the kitchen from the living room. Lucas tensed at the sight of his old friend.

"Sawyer." He nodded in greeting. "You heard?"

"The whole town has heard. You have any leads?"

Lucas shook his head, aware of the tension between himself and the man he'd considered a brother. Regret played deep inside him as he thought of the events that had put a strain on their relationship. Sawyer was one of Lucas's college buddies as well as a lifelong friend, but their relationship had been tested when Sawyer's wife had been murdered and Lucas had had to investigate Sawyer for the crime. Thankfully Sawyer had been innocent, but the strain still lingered. "What are you doing here?"

"I'm here to help. I can put up posters, talk to people, do whatever you need me to do," Sawyer said. Mariah entered the room, interrupting the conversation.

The hopeful look she sent Lucas broke his heart, because he had nothing to tell her that would make her feel any better. The momentary shine in her eyes dimmed. "Nothing?"

"Not yet. It looks like you've been busy while I've been gone."

"I've contacted everyone I can think of to get the word out that my son is missing. Somewhere in this town, somebody has to know what happened or at least have a piece of information that can help us find them." She raised her chin as if expecting a fight from him.

"It was a good idea," he said, and watched the breath ease out of her. She reached out and took Sawyer's hand. "Your friend here has been helping me print off posters from the computer. He's promised to see that they go up all over town." She released Sawyer's hand and instead clutched herself around the waist, as if she were physically holding herself together.

"I'm going to head out now." Sawyer turned his attention back to Lucas. "Anything else I can do?"

"Not that I can think of," Lucas replied.

"I'll just get those posters," Sawyer said to Mariah.

Lucas watched his friend head for the door. "Sawyer?" Sawyer turned back to face him. "Thanks."

Sawyer flashed him a smile that spoke of old bonds and years of friendship, and Lucas felt himself relax somewhat.

"I thought maybe you'd get some sleep while I was out," Lucas said to Mariah when Sawyer had left.

"I'll sleep when Billy is home safe and sound," she replied.

Although she hadn't slept, it was obvious she'd

showered and changed her clothes. Her shiny hair was neatly pulled back and held with a ponytail holder at the nape of her neck.

In all the time he'd known her, he'd never seen her in anything casual, but she now wore a pair of jeans that hugged her long slender legs and a sleeveless cotton blouse that was the same shade of blue as her eyes.

The casual clothing suited her, made her look less stern and more approachable and stirred a protective urge inside him that he hadn't felt for a woman in a very long time.

"Most of my neighbors have shown up to put out posters and search," she said as she moved to the coffeemaker on the countertop. "I did an interview with the local news, and they're going to show it this evening on the six-o'clock broadcast."

Their conversation was interrupted as Candy Tanner came into the kitchen. "I thought I heard your voice in here," she said to Lucas. "I need to talk to you about something." She shifted from foot to foot and looked as if she'd rather be anywhere else.

"About what?" Lucas looked at the young woman who was one of Jenny's closest friends. Her gaze shifted away from him, and a new tension rose up inside him. "You know something about what's going on, Candy?"

"No, not really, but I thought I should tell you that I know Jenny has been seeing Remy Troulous," she said.

Blood roared in Lucas's ears as he stared at Candy. "Seeing Remy Troulous? What do you mean? As in dating him?"

"No, I'm sure she wasn't dating him," Candy replied as she took a step back from Lucas. "But I know she had a meeting with him about something last week."

"What in the hell was she doing with Remy Troulous?"

"I don't know." Candy took another step backward. "She wouldn't tell me and she made me promise I wouldn't tell anyone, but I thought you should know." She turned and fled the kitchen as if afraid of Lucas's wrath.

"Who is Remy Troulous?" Mariah asked.

Lucas knew his reply would only add to the terror he knew she already felt for her son. "He's the head of a gang called the Voodoo Priests. He's not a good guy, Mariah."

She stared at him for a long moment. "And it's possible he has my son."

FROM THE MOMENT that dawn had broken, Mariah had felt as if she'd entered an alternate universe. But now, as she stared at Lucas, that universe took on a new nightmarish quality.

"The Voodoo Priests?" she repeated faintly. A new horror swept through her. She watched as he pulled his car keys out of his pocket. "Are you going to find this Remy?"

"I'm going to try."

"Wait, I'm coming with you."

Lucas's frown deepened. "I think it would be better if you stayed here."

His tone held the strong, authoritative note that she'd often heard him use with Jenny, and it sent a ripple of irritation through her. She embraced it, finding it so much easier to handle than the fear that gnawed at her with sharp teeth.

"And I think it would be best if I come with you. If

this Remy has Billy, then he's going to need me, and he's probably going to need his inhaler." She heard the anger that scorched her words and she drew a deep breath to gain control. "Billy is just a little boy. He'll need me."

He stared at her for a long moment, as if assessing his options, then gave her a curt nod. "Get what you need and let's get moving."

She hurried out of the kitchen and toward Billy's bedroom, her heart pounding with the anxious rhythm it had been beating all night long.

The house no longer felt like her home. People milled about, people she had called in the early-morning hours for help. But there seemed to be nothing anyone could do. It was as if a hole had opened up in the earth and swallowed Billy and Jenny whole.

Remy Troulous. What would a man like that want with Billy and Jenny? If their kidnapping was about a ransom, then why hadn't she or Lucas received a call demanding money?

She entered Billy's room and tried not to breathe in the little-boy scent of him that lingered there, knowing that if she dwelled on the smell of her son or the feel of his mouth against her cheek when he kissed her or the sound of his laughter, she'd lose it.

His pajamas were tossed on the bed. She didn't even know what he was wearing. She didn't know what he'd picked out to wear on the day he'd been kidnapped. Tears burned in her eyes, but she sucked them back, grabbed his inhaler, then hurried back to find Lucas getting people out of the house.

She pocketed the inhaler as her boss, Richard Welch,

approached her. He took her hands in his, his brown eyes radiating true sympathy. "Don't you worry about anything at the office," he said. "We'll manage without you until Billy is home safe and sound."

Mariah squeezed his hands. The mayor might be a self-absorbed big fish in a little pond most of the time, but the concern that radiated from his eyes at the moment was very real.

"Thank you, Richard. Hopefully he'll be home soon and things will go back to normal." Normal? Would anything ever be normal again? she wondered.

Lucas joined them, and Richard dropped Mariah's hands and turned to face him. "I trust you'll do everything in your power to find Billy and your sister. After the debacle with Sawyer Bennett and his wife's murder we don't need any more bad press." He frowned. "Murder, and now this kidnapping. Before long, Conja Creek will have a reputation for being a crime pit. We don't want that to happen. I want this tied up as soon as possible."

Lucas eyed Richard as if he were a creature from another planet. "Our goals are the same, Mayor." Lucas's voice radiated his tension.

"You'll keep me informed?" Richard asked.

"Of course," Lucas replied.

"If nothing breaks before tomorrow we'll set up a press conference to ease the concerns of our citizens," Richard said.

Lucas nodded, his irritation with the man obvious in his clenched jaw and narrowed gaze. Mariah touched his arm. "We're wasting time. Shouldn't we be going?" All she wanted was to find the man who might have her son.

"Absolutely," Lucas replied.

With Deputy Ben Rankell left at the house to man the phone and encourage people to leave, Lucas and Mariah walked outside. The brilliant sunshine burned her eyes as they headed for his car. The night of worry and no sleep weighed heavily on her shoulders, but she shoved the exhaustion away.

"I'll never understand how that man managed to get elected," Lucas said as he started his engine.

"Because underneath all his posturing and grandstanding is a good heart," she replied. "He cares about Conja Creek." She didn't want to talk about Lucas's issues with the mayor, which as far as she was concerned rose out of the fact that each man attempted to control the other. "Tell me about Remy Troulous," she said.

Her stomach clenched as she saw his hands tighten on the steering wheel.

"He's twenty-eight years old and has been in and out of jail a dozen times on different charges, mostly drugs. I've long suspected that he and his gang run drugs up from Florida, but I haven't been able to prove anything." His frown intensified. "If I wanted to arrange my own kidnapping for one reason or another, Remy or one of his gangbangers is who I would talk to."

She looked at him without hiding a new irritation that swept through her. "You still really believe that Jenny is responsible for this? You might have raised your sister, but you sure don't know anything about her."

"And after two months of living with her, you know it all?"

"I know that the only real problem Jenny has is too much of you." She hadn't meant to start a fight, but her emotions were too close to the surface and she'd watched Lucas mentally browbeat Jenny too many times.

"What are you talking about?" He cast her a sharp glance.

What are you doing, Mariah? a little voice whispered inside her head. She realized it wasn't the time or her place to get into this, that she had enough problems at the moment without berating the very man who was trying to help her find her son. "Never mind. So, where do we find this Remy Troulous?"

He shot her another glance, one that told her he was going to let her words go…for now. "I'm not sure. I know his official address is with his grandmother, but he's rarely there. Still, that's where we'll start."

As he headed down Main Street, she stared out the side window, a thousand thoughts filling her head. She'd done a television interview and hoped that stations around the area picked it up.

But she also knew that if Frank had had nothing to do with Billy's disappearance and he saw the interview on television, then he would know for certain where she and Billy had landed after they'd run from Shreveport.

The idea of facing her ex-husband again sent not only icy chills through her but also years of bad memories. And it was those memories, she knew, that had prompted her to attack Lucas about his treatment of Jenny.

She reached into her pocket and touched the inhaler. *Billy,* her heart cried. *Where are you?* She'd face a million Franks if it meant getting her son back.

Her heart pounded so fast, so painfully in her chest that she wondered if she were on the verge of a heart attack.

"When we get to Georgia's place, it would be best if you stayed in the car," he said, breaking into her despairing thoughts.

There he went again, telling her what was best for her, just like he did his sister all the time. *Lucas knows best.* He knew what Jenny should eat, what she should wear, where she should get a job—it was no wonder Jenny floundered around, trying to figure out who she was. Lucas had never given her the independence to find out.

She bit her bottom lip, wondering why she was thinking about such things. She supposed her mind was seeking anything to puzzle over other than the horror of her missing son. If she allowed herself to think about Billy for too long, her thoughts took her to dark places and she felt as if she'd lose her mind.

She glanced over at Lucas, who was focused on maneuvering the narrow road. She'd always thought he was a handsome man, with his dark hair and dark eyes. He radiated a strength of purpose, a self-confidence that could be irritating. At the moment, she found it comforting.

He was a smart man, a good sheriff, and he had a vested interest in solving the case. Jenny. No matter what issues she had with the way he treated his sister, she'd never doubted that he loved Jenny.

For the first time, she realized that maybe the reason he wanted to believe that Jenny had orchestrated this was he feared for her if she hadn't.

"She's stronger than you think," she said softly.

He looked at her again, and for just a moment she saw naked emotion shining from his eyes. Fear, anger and guilt, they were all there for a mere second, then gone as if shutters had closed to block out the light.

"I just can't imagine what she was doing meeting with a man like Troulous."

"When we find them, you can ask her," she replied as he pulled up in front of a small shanty.

She didn't intend to follow his suggestion that she remain in the car. Mariah figured if Remy's grandmother knew anything about Billy's kidnapping it wouldn't hurt to appeal to her, woman to woman.

She waited until Lucas was halfway up the porch, then she left the car and hurried after him. He showed his displeasure with her only in the tightening of his strong jaw as he knocked on the screen door.

Tension welled up inside Mariah, momentarily shoving away her exhaustion. She fought the impulse to grab hold of Lucas's arm, wondering what even prompted the urge.

A little old woman appeared at the door, her dark eyes suspicious as she saw Lucas. "He ain't here," she said without preamble.

"You don't even know why I'm here, Georgia," Lucas replied.

"I know when the sheriff shows up on my doorstep it's because he's looking for Remy, and Remy ain't here. I haven't seen him for a week." Her words caused Mariah's heart to sink.

"You know where he might be? Is he bunking with a girlfriend?" Lucas asked.

Georgia shook her head. "Who knows. What's he done now? Last time I saw him he told me he was trying to get his life together. Told me he was tired of gangbanging and such." The old woman seemed to shrink in size as misery darkened her eyes. "I should have known not to believe him."

"Please, Mrs. Troulous, can you think of anyplace we might find him? It's important. I have a little boy who is missing."

One of Georgia's gray eyebrows lifted. "You looking for the wrong person. Remy might be guilty of many things, but he'd never harm a child."

"I still need to talk to him," Lucas said. "If you see him before I do, tell him I'm looking for him."

Georgia nodded, and together Mariah and Lucas returned to his car. "What now?" she asked. "Surely you have an idea where this Remy might be. We've got to find him. He's the only lead we have."

Lucas started the car engine and puffed out a deep sigh. "I know dozens of places he might be."

"Then we start at the first place and don't stop until we find him." She couldn't stand the idea of another night passing without Billy being home with her.

The afternoon passed with failure after failure as Lucas checked all the known friends and places where Remy might be. Nobody had seen him—or, at least, nobody would admit to it.

Lucas checked with all his deputies throughout the day, but nobody had anything to report.

At two, Wally called Lucas to tell him that an FBI agent had arrived. Lucas and Mariah drove to the office and met with Michael Kessler, a young, earnest agent who listened to the facts of the case dispassionately, then indicated that he'd be doing his own investigation and would appreciate the support of Lucas and his deputies.

"Only one agent?" Mariah said as they drove away from the sheriff's office. "They only sent one man?"

"He'll have more resources than we have," Lucas replied. "Besides, even if they sent a hundred agents, we won't get any answers without a viable lead."

At seven they grabbed hamburgers at a local drive-through. Even though food was the last thing on her mind, Mariah ate, knowing that if she didn't, she'd make herself sick.

Was somebody feeding Billy? Or was he hungry and scared and crying for her? The last of her burger remained uneaten as haunting thoughts filled her head.

They were still parked in the drive-through when Lucas's cell phone rang. Mariah's hope instantly soared. Maybe Billy and Jenny had been found. He answered and she watched the play of emotion on his face as he listened to the caller.

"We'll be right there," he said, then hung up and turned to look at her.

The hope that had momentarily buoyed her up inside crashed back down to earth as she saw the shadows that darkened his eyes. "We need to get back to your place," he said. "There's been another phone call."

Chapter Four

"I don't know if it's a crank or not," Wally said as Lucas and Mariah walked through her front door. "I've got it taped and I checked the number the call came from with the phone company. It was the pay phone behind Jimbo's gas station. I already called Jimbo to see if he saw anyone using the phone, but no one did. I also sent Maylor over there to check out the phone and try to lift some prints."

Lucas had little hope that the caller had been dumb enough to leave prints, and he wasn't surprised that nobody had seen anyone using the phone. The area behind Jimbo's was filled with old wrecked cars and used tires. It was more a junkyard than anything else, and Lucas figured few people even knew there was a phone back there.

"Let's hear it," he said, and gestured to the recording equipment.

Mariah leaned against one of the kitchen chairs, her face as pale as paper as she stared at the phone. He couldn't believe the strength she'd exhibited so far. Most women would be in the care of a physician, swallowing tranquilizers to get through the ordeal. She'd definitely earned his respect.

Wally punched the Play button and his voice filled the air. "Harrington's residence," his taped greeting said.

"I know the sheriff isn't there, and I have no desire to talk to you, so just give him this message." The voice was low, a guttural whisper. It was the same person who had called Lucas on his cell phone.

"A game isn't fun unless two can play. I'll give you a little clue for the day. They're safe in a place where no one can hear, where the cries of the dead ring loud and clear." The caller paused. "Tell Sheriff Jamison to send his men home, to send everyone home. I don't like extra players in my game. Tell him I'm watching his every move and trust me, he doesn't want to break my rules." There was an ominous tone to the already creepy voice.

"Listen, why don't you—" Wally's reply was cut off by an audible click as the caller hung up.

For a moment the three of them said nothing, but simply continued to stare at the machine, as if answers to their questions were forthcoming.

It was Mariah who broke the silence. She drew in a deep breath and met Lucas's gaze. "He said they were safe and sound." Her voice trembled slightly but also held the hope of a woman grasping at anything.

"That's what he said," Lucas replied. There was no way he was going to tell her that the word of a kidnapper wasn't the most reliable in the world.

Mariah turned her gaze to Wally. "You have to go. You heard what he said, he wants everyone to leave and he's watching us. I don't want anyone here except me and Lucas."

Wally looked at Lucas, his forehead wrinkled into a hundred frown lines. Lucas felt the weight of his next decision in the very pit of his gut where tension burned with hot flames. Although he didn't want to play games with a criminal, he was also aware that he wasn't willing to gamble with Billy's and Jenny's lives.

"Wally, head back to the office and keep all the men away from here. Let Agent Kessler know what's going on. I'll be in touch with each of you on my cell phone."

"Are you sure?" Wally asked.

Lucas nodded. "I can't risk not playing by his rules, at least for the moment."

Dusk was deepening into night as Lucas walked Wally to his patrol car. "I've got Louis checking out Phil Ribideaux. The rest of you try to locate Remy Troulous. If you find him, bring him in and call me. Keep questioning whoever you think might have any information that might help us find Billy and Jenny. It would help if we could find somebody that saw them yesterday. Keep me posted on progress. I'm putting you in charge of coordinating things from the office. Make nice with Agent Kessler. If he needs anything, see that he gets it, but just make sure all the men stay away from here."

Wally nodded. "Anything else?"

"Yeah, see what you can dig up on a Frank Landers, last known address in Shreveport. The authorities there haven't been able to locate him, but I'm not sure how hard they're looking. And check around, see if anyone has noticed any strangers hanging around lately."

"Got it," Wally said.

Lucas watched Wally drive away. He stood for several minutes in the driveway and stared around the area. *Tell him I'm watching his every move and he doesn't want to break my rules.*

The people who lived on this street were good hard-working people who valued family and friends. He knew these people…or did he?

Suddenly every drapery drawn at a window might hide a kidnapper, every closed door implied secrets. Was somebody watching from next door? Across the street?

With a sigh he returned to the kitchen where Mariah was seated at the table, playing the message again. She pushed the Stop button when he came in. "The clue. I've been thinking about it." Even though the timing was completely inappropriate, he couldn't help but notice how pretty she looked with her hair coming loose and springing around her shoulders and her cheeks filled with color that had been lacking for most of the day.

"What about it?"

"He said they're where the cries of the dead ring loud and clear. It's got to be the cemetery, Lucas. Maybe they're in a crypt. We've got to go there and check it out."

"Whoa. We aren't going anywhere. I'll go and take a look around."

"If you think I'm going to stay here, you're crazy," she replied. "I can either ride with you or I can take my own car, but one way or another, I'm going to the cemetery. That's where the clue leads and that's where I need to be."

"It could be dangerous," Lucas protested. "You

know that even under the best of circumstances the cemetery isn't a good place to hang out, especially at night."

She stepped closer to him and placed a hand on his arm. This close he could see that her blue eyes had silver flecks. Those eyes pleaded with him. "Lucas, please. I have to go with you. It's my son. I don't care about any danger. This is the first real clue we've had. Don't make me fight you on this."

He tried to imagine somebody trying to keep him from going to find Jenny. There was nobody on the face of the earth who could stop him—and he wouldn't be the one to stop her.

"All right, then, let's go."

Minutes later they were in his car heading toward the north side of town where the Conja Creek Cemetery was located. His car beams penetrated the deepening darkness, and tension coiled like a snake in the pit of his stomach.

"We could be walking into a setup," he said.

"What kind of a setup? If somebody wanted to kill either you or me, they could have done so without all this drama," she said. "If we're the targets, then why involve Jenny and Billy?"

He tightened his hands on the steering wheel. "I don't know. I can't get a handle on this." The words fell from him involuntarily, and he hit the steering wheel with his palm. "He's obviously playing with us and I don't know why. This is probably nothing more than a wild-goose chase."

"Don't say that," she exclaimed with fervor. "Right now my hope is the only thing holding me together. Please don't take that away from me."

He glanced in her direction. "You're one of the strongest women I think I've ever met. Most women would be basket cases by now."

"I've had to be strong to survive the choices I've made in my life."

Again he realized how little he knew about her, and new interest stirred inside him. "Bad choices?"

"Only one. I married the wrong man. Why aren't you married, Lucas?"

"I was once. I'd just graduated college and gotten married when my mother died. Jenny was twelve, and so I moved back to the family home with my new bride. The marriage lasted for six months, then Kerry told me she hadn't applied for the job of helping to raise a twelve-year-old. She gave me an ultimatum—make other arrangements for Jenny, or she was leaving. I helped her pack."

"I'm sorry it didn't work out for you," she said.

He offered her a tight smile. "I'm not. Oh, it hurt at the time, but I hadn't realized until that moment how selfish Kerry was. She definitely wasn't the kind of woman I wanted to spend the rest of my life with."

"And there hasn't been anyone since?"

He wasn't sure if she was really interested or if she was just making conversation to keep her thoughts off their destination and the high stakes involved.

"Jenny has managed to take up most of my time and energy. There's never been much left for anyone else."

"Jenny has been an adult for a while now. Don't you think it's time you give her less time and attention?"

"I think the reasons we're here now put to rest the idea that Jenny doesn't require my time and attention," he replied dryly.

"You still think Jenny had something to do with all this?" Her voice held an edge of exasperation.

He didn't answer for several long seconds. Mostly because he wasn't sure what was in his heart. He desperately wanted to believe that Jenny was nothing more than an innocent victim, but he just wasn't sure.

"Jenny doesn't always make the best choices in her life," he finally said.

"From what I've seen, Jenny rarely makes *any* choices in her life," she countered. "You make them all for her."

He cast her a sharp, sideways glance. "Are you trying to pick a fight with me?"

She flushed and looked down at her clenched hands. "No. I'm sorry. Your relationship with Jenny is really none of my business."

There was something in her tone, a vague disapproval that made him want to continue the conversation, but at that moment the rusted ironwork of the gates to the cemetery appeared in his high beams.

Conja Creek Cemetery was like dozens of other Louisiana burial grounds. Sun-bleached tombs rose up from the earth, some simple square structures, others like miniature houses complete with fencing around them.

There was no caretaker living on-site, and the cemetery was on the edge of town with no surrounding houses or buildings.

"I'll get the gate," he said as he put his car in Park. He pulled his gun as he got out of the car, his eyes scanning the area and his ears listening for any sound that didn't belong.

The gate screeched in protest as he opened it, announcing to anyone who might be inside that they had arrived. He stared inside the gate to the narrow rows that led between the structures. Cities of the dead, that's what people called the cemeteries in Louisiana. He just hoped this particular city of the dead didn't hold the bodies of Billy and Jenny.

MARIAH DIDN'T THINK her heart could hurt as much as it did as Lucas pulled the car through the cemetery gates and parked in the space provided just inside.

Was Billy here? In one of the tombs? She reached her hand in her pocket and touched his inhaler, as if it were a talisman that would lead her to him.

She was light-headed and sick to her stomach, a combination of too much coffee and too little sleep. She just wanted her baby back home where he belonged.

"You stay in the car. I'll check things out," he said as he turned off the car engine.

"I'm not staying in the car," she replied. "If you find them, and Billy is in a full asthma attack, he's going to need immediate medical attention. I didn't come all this way with you to sit in the car." She opened her car door and ignored his muttered curse.

The night air was thick, hot and steamy, and for a moment she leaned against the car door and tried to imagine Billy in this place of death. The very atmosphere itself would work against him, so thick and sultry. Add fear and stress, and he could be in real physical danger.

Lucas joined her and put an arm around her shoulder. For a moment she leaned into him, drawing from his strength. She might not like the way he treated his sister, but at the moment she couldn't think of anyone else she wanted by her side.

"Stay close to me," he whispered. "We don't know what we're walking into."

She straightened and nodded as he once again pulled his gun. Together they left the car and headed for the first "street" between tombs.

"Billy!" The scream tore from Mariah's throat. She waited to hear an answer, but there was nothing.

The area was lit with small electric lights low to the ground, the illumination creating a contrast of eerie shadows. They walked slowly and checked each tomb to see if one might hold a sign that Billy and Jenny were inside.

"Billy, are you here?" Over and over Mariah cried out, desperate to hear the sound of her son's voice.

Lucas moved slowly, cautiously. He'd take a few steps then stop and cock his head, as if listening. The only thing she heard was the buzz of mosquitoes and the continuous click of insects.

Billy, where are you? Her heart screamed as loud as her mouth.

"Jenny, are you here? Make a sound, give us a clue, do something to show us you're here," Lucas called.

Mariah had never been afraid of places. Scary movies didn't bother her. Spiders, snakes and gators didn't concern her. The only fear she'd ever felt was of the man she had married. Frank.

Was he behind all this? Certainly a sadistic game of hide-and-seek wasn't out of character. One of the deputies had called Lucas earlier to let him know that her news story had been picked up by the wire services.

If Frank wasn't behind this, and if he'd been watching television and had seen her, then he would know that she and Billy were in Conja Creek. She rubbed her left wrist— the wrist that he'd broken on the day she'd left him.

The thought of seeing him again sent a shiver of fear through her and she moved closer to Lucas, as if he could keep all the boogeymen out of her life.

As they continued to search, the hope that had filled her began to waver. Had they perceived the clue incorrectly? *Where the cries of the dead ring loud and clear,* that's what the caller had said. Where else could that be but a cemetery, and this was the only cemetery in the town of Conja Creek.

When they reached the last wide aisle between the tombs, despair quickly usurped hope. And when they reached the last tomb on that aisle, the strength that had been holding her together vanished.

She fell to her knees, unable to take another step as the grief that she'd been shoving away since the moment she'd awakened from her nap and found Billy gone rushed in to consume her.

Tears blinded her, and she was unable to control the deep, wrenching sobs that ripped from her throat. She collapsed to the ground, vaguely aware of Lucas holstering his gun and bending down beside her.

"I know," he whispered as he physically pulled her into his arms. "Shh." He stroked her hair as she continued to sob, unable to stop.

"They were supposed to be here," she cried. "Damn him. Damn whoever has them, for putting us through this." She clung to Lucas, surprised to find his arms provided the comfort she needed.

As she remained in his embrace, she became aware of the frantic beating of his heart against her own. She realized at that moment that his despair was as great as her own, his disappointment was as black as the one that filled her.

She raised her head and looked at him through her veil of tears. His eyes held the same rage that filled her, a rage at the man who had brought them here, the man who had ripped the very fabric of her soul.

"Jenny didn't do this," he said, his voice hoarse with emotion. "She'd never put us through this."

"That's what I've been trying to tell you," Mariah replied. She could tell by the dawning horror in his eyes that the realization that Jenny was in terrible trouble was just now sinking in.

"Come on, let's get out of here," he said, his voice filled with rough emotion. He stood and held out his hand to help her up off the ground.

She had just stood when a crack split the air and Lucas threw himself at her, tumbling her to the ground as he covered her body with his.

Chapter Five

Lucas couldn't tell where the gunshot had come from, but he heard the ping as the bullet hit the tomb behind where they had just been standing.

His first impulse was to protect Mariah, and as he lay on top of her, adrenaline pumped through him. He tightened his hold on his gun as he scanned the area.

Dammit, there were too many shadows where a shooter could hide, too many trees and tombs for him to discern the hint of a person. The shot had caused a cessation to the insect noise, but as the minutes ticked by the cacophony of bugs resumed.

As time passed, in the back of his mind he became more aware of Mariah. Her hand grasped the front of his shirt, as if she was afraid he might jump up and run away. Her heartbeat raced against his own, and despite the circumstances, he couldn't help but notice the softness of her lush curves under his body.

Irritated by his lapse in concentration, he rose to a crouch above her. "Stay here and stay down," he commanded. "I'm going to take a look around."

She tightened her grip on his shirt and in the faint

moonlight her eyes shone more silver than blue. "Be careful. He could still be out there." She reluctantly released her hold on him.

Still in a low crouch, Lucas moved away from her, toward the area where he thought the shot might have come from. He didn't think the shooter was still there.

In fact, he didn't think the shooter was still in the cemetery. It was a gut feeling coupled with the knowledge that if the man had wanted to kill one of them, he could have with that single shot.

He might have missed because he was a terrible shot, but Lucas didn't think so. He thought the bullet had missed them because it was just another game the kidnapper was playing. He was taking pleasure in terrorizing them.

He straightened to his full height, making himself an easy target, but no other shots were fired. He walked back to where Mariah was still lying on the ground.

"I think he's gone." He held out a hand to help her up.

"Are you sure?" She didn't move from her prone position.

"As sure as I can be. If he wanted to hurt us, he could have shot us at any time while we were searching the area." He grimaced. "I think that shot was just a playful reminder that we aren't the ones in charge of this game."

She slipped her small hand in his and he pulled her up. "They aren't here, are they? Billy and Jenny aren't here and that clue was just part of his stupid game."

He nodded. "Let's get the hell out of here."

It was a long walk back to the car. Lucas kept his gun ready and every muscle tense as he watched for danger that didn't come.

They got into the car and he started the engine, immediately turning on the air conditioner to relieve the sweltering heat and humidity.

As he pulled out of the cemetery, neither of them said a word. The adrenaline that had surged inside him eased away, leaving him not only exhausted but also defenseless against the dark thoughts in his mind.

Jenny. Pain seared through him as he thought of his sister. He'd spent all his adult life trying to protect her, both from herself and from others. He'd tried to guide her, to make her better than she was, better than the mother who had given her life.

"Are you okay?" Mariah's soft, weary voice pulled him from his thoughts.

"As okay as you are," he replied.

"Then you aren't okay," she said with a surprising touch of dry humor.

"No, I'm not," he agreed. "I'm frustrated and worried and I don't think this is about a ransom anymore."

"Then what is it about?" she asked.

Lucas frowned and tightened his hands on the steering wheel. "I think it's personal. I think the perpetrator wants one of us to be afraid, to suffer."

She leaned her head back and closed her eyes. "Then he's succeeded."

Those were the last words spoken for the remainder of the drive home. When they arrived at her place, the first thing Lucas did was check the phone messages as Mariah got them each a bottle of water from the fridge.

The first message was from Mayor Richard Welch. "Lucas, I've heard through the grapevine that you've sent your men home, but Billy and Jenny are still missing. I hope you know what you're doing. I need to be updated and maybe we need to put our heads together to see what's the best way to deal with this situation. The public deserves to know what's going on in this community."

Lucas puffed out a sigh. "I wish he'd spend his time governing the town instead of trying to govern me."

Mariah sank into a seat at the table, her weariness evident in the slump of her shoulders and the hollowness of her eyes. "He's just trying to be helpful." She unscrewed the lid on her water and took a long, deep drink.

"It would be helpful if he'd just leave me to the job of upholding the law."

The next three messages were from neighbors, offering to cook, offering to help. Another two were from reporters looking for an interview. The next message shot a new burst of adrenaline through Lucas.

"Touching scene in the cemetery." The familiar voice filled the room. "Is she consoling you, or are you consoling her?" The sound of insects was background noise. "A minute ago I stood so close to you both that I could see the sweat on Lucas's forehead and I could smell that flowery perfume that Mariah wears."

Mariah jumped as the sound of a shot filled the room. The sound was followed by a low laugh. "I could have killed you just now," he said. "I'll be in touch."

The line went dead.

Mariah released a loud gasp. "He was watching us as we searched. He was there all along." Emotion choked her voice and she backhanded her water bottle off the table, unmindful of the water that spilled across the floor. She jumped up, her eyes wild. "What kind of person does something like this? What kind of monster is he?"

"I don't know." But there were things Lucas needed to do, and with that in mind he pulled his cell phone from his pocket and punched in the number at the sheriff's office.

"Ben, first thing in the morning I need you to check out the cemetery for me. Somebody took a shot at Mariah and me out there tonight. I want you to see if you can locate the bullet." He quickly explained to his deputy where they had been standing when the gun had been fired and where he thought Ben would find the bullet. It would at least tell them what kind of gun it came from.

The next call he made was to Ed Maylor. "Ed, did I wake you?"

"Nah, I was just sitting here watching the boob tube. What's up?"

"I was wondering if you could do me a favor. Would you run by my place and tell Marquette to give you my overnight bag and a couple of clean uniforms, then meet me at the station with them?" He looked at Mariah, who stood with her back to him as she stared out the window into the night. "I'm going to be here at Mariah's until this is resolved."

"Sure. When do you want to meet?"

"An hour."

The last call was to Deputy Louis DuBois. "Where are you, Louis?" he asked when the man answered his cell phone.

There was a long pause. "I'm in my car between Magnolia and Main. Uh, I'm looking for Phil Ribideaux."

"What do you mean you're looking for him?" Lucas asked.

"Uh, I seem to have lost him."

Lucas closed his eyes and squeezed the phone more tightly against his ear. "What do you mean you lost him?"

"I'm sorry, Lucas, but he got into that little sports car of his and he must have seen me behind him because he took off around a couple of corners and was gone."

"How long has it been since you had him in visual contact?" Lucas asked.

"At least an hour," Louis confessed. "I'm heading toward his house now to see if he's returned there."

"Keep me posted." Lucas clicked off and muttered a curse.

Mariah turned to face him. "What's happened?"

"I had Louis following Phil Ribideaux, and apparently in the past hour he lost him."

She leaned against the wall and brushed a strand of her unruly curly hair away from her face. "An hour. That means it's possible it was Phil Ribideaux who was in the cemetery."

"It's also possible it was a dozen other people," Lucas replied. "In truth, I can't imagine Phillip Ribideaux having the imagination or the balls to pull something like this off." He pulled his keys from his pocket. "Look, I need to go down to the station. Will you be okay alone for a little while?"

Her gaze went to the telephone. "What if he calls again?"

"I don't think he will, at least not again tonight. I think he's had his fun for now." He frowned. Funny…

all the people who had shown up that morning had been well-meaning neighbors, but there had been no phone calls, no appearance of anyone who seemed to be Mariah's close friend. "Is there somebody I can call to be here with you? Maybe a good friend?"

She shook her head. "Jenny was becoming a good friend, but other than her I have no close friends here," she replied. "Between my job and Billy, there hasn't been time for fostering any real friendships." She rubbed her left wrist. "Besides, I'm a private person. Friends want to know where you come from and where you're going. I didn't want to talk about the first and I don't have answers for the second."

She turned back to face the window. "Go do whatever it is you need to do. I'll be fine here."

She might be fine, but he was an emotional wreck as he drove to his office. Despite the lateness of the hour, he'd called Wally and told him to gather the deputies for a briefing. He also wanted to coordinate with Agent Kessler.

As he drove, his head filled with thoughts of Jenny. He'd clung to the perverse hope that somehow she was behind her own disappearance, that she wasn't in serious danger other than getting a butt-chewing from him when she finally showed up.

But as they'd walked the cemetery, he'd realized Mariah was right. Jenny might not mind making him worry himself sick, but she'd never do something like this to Mariah. She'd never keep Billy away from his mother.

However, it was possible that Jenny's bad choices in friends and relationships had put her in this position. Remy Troulous was one of those bad choices. What the hell had she been doing with him? And where the hell was Remy Troulous now?

Lucas knew it was useless to search for the man. He was like a swamp rat, able to scurry through darkness and hide in any number of holes. He wouldn't be found unless he wanted to be, and there was no way to know when he'd decide to make an appearance.

Did Remy have anything to do with this? Or was it possible Phil Ribideaux was behind it? And what about the mysterious Frank Landers? The questions served no purpose other than to give him a headache and intensify his weariness.

He was going to have to get some sleep. He was running on empty and there was no way he could be sharp and focused, either physically or mentally, without rest.

The sheriff's office was in a building smack-dab in the middle of Main Street. He parked in the space allotted to him, then went inside where his deputies and the FBI agent awaited.

They all looked as tired as he felt. It didn't take long for him to fill them in on what had happened at the cemetery, then listen to each of them report on what they'd been doing in the past few hours. None of them had anything substantial to report.

The Shreveport authorities had still been unable to locate Frank Landers, Remy Troulous was missing in action, as was Phil Ribideaux. Further interrogations of Mariah's neighbors had yielded nothing, and by the time Lucas left the office with his overnight bag and clean clothes in hand, he carried with him an overwhelming sense of frustration.

The first forty-eight hours after a crime was committed were crucial, and Lucas was aware that they knew little more than they had in the first hours after Billy and Jenny had disappeared. He and his men were doing everything they could to find Jenny and Billy, but at the moment the kidnapper was definitely in charge.

Eventually he would make a mistake. Lucas had no doubt about that. The phone calls told Lucas that the kidnapper wanted to brag, needed to connect, and eventually he'd make a mistake. But until that happened Lucas could only react, and he hated not being in control.

He told his deputies that he would stay at Mariah's house, since the kidnapper was calling on her home phone. He would be the only law enforcement agent there. For now, he was playing by the kidnapper's rules. He and his deputies would stay in touch by phone and continue to meet at regular intervals at the office.

Although Conja Creek wasn't a hotbed of criminal activity, they still had to contend with the usual crimes that occurred on a regular basis. He put Ed Maylor in charge of coordinating with the citizens who wanted to help find Jenny and Billy and put Wally in charge of the office while Lucas stayed at Mariah's. Agent Kessler would coordinate with the state police and continue to work with the deputies to interview and assess the situation.

Kessler indicated that he was more than willing to call in several more agents, but Lucas feared the wrath of the kidnapper if too many law enforcement agents appeared in town. He and Kessler agreed that for the short term everything would remain status quo.

When he arrived back at Mariah's, he walked through the front door and was met with silence. He dropped his bag and his clothes on the sofa, then went in search of Mariah.

He found her in Billy's room, curled up in a fetal position on the bed. She clutched her son's yellow-and-navy pajamas to her chest, and his heart clenched at the sight.

Her sleep was obviously deep, for she didn't move as he approached her. She must have showered after he left, and changed her clothes, for she now wore a pair of jogging pants and a different T-shirt.

For a long moment he stood and watched her, his heart clenching once again as he saw the dark shadows beneath her long lashes, the faint crease that rode her brow, as if even sleep hadn't offered her the escape she needed.

He wanted to curl up beside her in the bed, take her into his arms and hold her and fill his head with the sweet scent of her. The desire shocked him. With all that was going on, how was it possible that desire managed to rear its unwelcome head?

Maybe because it was a familiar, known emotion as opposed to the unfamiliar torment of fear that rocked through him as his heart cried his sister's name. But, Mariah Harrington had touched him in places he hadn't been touched in a very long time.

Her strength amazed him, her courage awed him and the secrets he sensed she had from her past intrigued him. She was like no other woman he had encountered in a very long time.

He spied a navy afghan folded over the chair at the desk and he grabbed it and gently laid it over her. The house was cool and he wanted to do something, anything that felt like taking care of her.

He was grateful that she was asleep, glad that he wouldn't have to tell her the instructions he'd given his deputies. He left the bedroom and went into the kitchen, where he stood at the window and stared into the black of night.

This was the second night. Almost forty-eight hours had passed since Jenny and Billy had been taken. What were the odds that somebody had kidnapped them and was keeping them alive in a secret place here in Conja Creek? He figured slim to none.

That's why he was glad Mariah was sleeping. So he wouldn't have to tell her that he suspected they were now looking for Jenny's and Billy's bodies.

NIGHT HAD FALLEN AGAIN, and with it the terror of the darkness, the horror of the unknown. Jenny cradled Billy's head in her lap, worried as she heard the sound of his labored breathing.

He was asleep, but it was a fitful rest, and she could only guess at the bad dreams a frightened eight-year-old little boy might suffer.

His breathing worried her. She knew how bad Billy's asthma could get. Twice in the couple of months she'd lived with Mariah, he'd had to be rushed to the emergency room because his nebulizer hadn't been able to give him the relief he'd needed.

Although it wasn't critical yet, she feared what another day away from his mommy, away from his home might bring. As his stress and fear level rose, so did his breathing issues.

Dawn had brought a new level of understanding to Jenny and a heightened sense of simmering fear.

As light had crept in around the cracks in the boards of the structure where they were being held, she'd been able to see that it was a small room built with new, strong wood. The nails—thick, big spikes—were driven in deep and sound.

Besides the mattress on the floor, in one corner was a portable potty and in the other corner was a wooden shelf filled with nonperishable food. There were boxes of breakfast bars and crackers, beef jerky and canned goods with pop lids. Beneath the shelf were cases of bottled water.

It was the plethora of food that frightened her more than anything. Whoever had them had prepared for them to be here a long time. Why? What in God's name could they want?

She racked her brain, trying to figure out who would want to kidnap them and why. But she had no answers. It might be about money. Certainly Lucas could afford to pay a huge ransom for their release. In fact, Jenny had her own trust fund that contained enough to make a kidnapper happy for the rest of his life.

When Billy had awakened, they'd both screamed for help, hoping somebody would hear and come to rescue them. But it was as if they were yelling at the bottom of the ocean. Nobody replied. Nobody came.

When they'd exhausted themselves screaming, she'd spent most of the rest of the day examining their surroundings, trying to find a weakness she could exploit to get them out of there. But there didn't seem to be any way out.

She'd finally given up and had played games with Billy. They'd played I Spy and an alphabet game, then had played Rock, Paper, Scissors until she thought she'd go mad.

As dusk had approached and Billy's anxiety began to increase, Jenny had tried to entertain him by talking about the animals who lived in the swamps. Billy loved to learn, and Jenny had once thought about being a teacher. But when she'd gone to college, she'd taken business instead of education classes, because Lucas had thought that would be a smarter choice.

Tears now filled her eyes as she thought of her older brother. He could be bossy and a know-it-all, but she adored him. He'd been her hero for most of her life, fixing messes she made and taking care of her.

Lately she'd been angry with him, wanting him to back off and let her live her own life. She wanted to make her own choices and figure things out on her own, but sometimes she felt so stupid.

She leaned her head back against the wooden wall and stroked her fingers through Billy's hair. She'd always loved kids, and Billy had found a special place in her heart.

He coughed and she recognized the tight bark as his asthma cough. She closed her eyes, terror once again filling her.

Billy needed to get out of here before his breathing grew worse. But she couldn't physically break through the wooden walls that kept them prisoner. She couldn't even try to negotiate with their kidnapper because, since the moment they had awakened from whatever had knocked them out, they had been utterly alone.

She'd been on the verge of tears all day, but had refused to allow them to fall because she knew it would upset Billy. But now, in the darkness and with Billy asleep, tears trickled down her cheeks. She must have done something stupid, something to put herself at risk. She wasn't sure what it had been, but somehow this had to be her fault.

She needed her brother to find them. She needed Lucas to be her hero one last time, then she swore to herself that she'd never do anything stupid again.

Chapter Six

Sleep fell away in increments. Mariah became aware of the faint sound of chirping birds drifting through the windowpane, and for just a moment a sense of well-being filled her.

Then she opened her eyes and realized she was in Billy's bed, and reality slammed into her a like a sledge-hammer crushing her heart.

Another dawn, and he was still not home. She squeezed her eyes shut as a rush of emotion filled her. She could only assume that nothing had happened while she slept, for if it had, Lucas would have awakened her.

How was she going to get through another day... another minute of the tormenting fear? How was she going to survive her next breath not knowing where her son was or if he were alive or—

She gasped, not wanting to even think that she might never see Billy's smile again, would never hear that silly giggle of his.

Drawing a deep breath, she took in the scent of him that lingered in his room, the faint Billy fragrance that clung to his little pajamas. How long before that Billy smell went away? Would he be gone so long that there would be nothing left of him?

Needing to escape her own thoughts, she hurried into the bathroom where she washed her face, brushed her teeth and pulled her hair back with a ponytail holder at the nape of her neck.

She looked tired despite the sleep she'd gotten. Of course, much of her sleep had been haunted by dreams of Billy crying for her, needing her, and she'd been unable to go to him.

She was living every mother's nightmare. She'd read the tragic news stories of missing children, had seen parents on the television years after the disappearance still seeking answers. She didn't want to be one of those parents. She didn't want to think that Billy might be a statistic.

Shoving away the horrible thoughts, she went in search of Lucas.

She found him stretched out on his back on her sofa. He was sound asleep. He wore a pair of worn jeans and a white T-shirt and she realized it was the first time she'd seen him out of his khaki uniform.

He looked good in jeans, and the T-shirt pulled across the width of his chest. She had always been attracted to Lucas. From the first time he'd strode into the office demanding to speak to the mayor, she'd felt a magnetic spark.

But he scared her more than a little bit. He reminded her of the husband she'd fled. She'd already made one major mistake in her life, and she had the feeling that following through on her attraction to

Lucas Jamison would simply be another monumental mistake.

He must have been exhausted, for the lamp on the end table closest to his head burned bright but didn't seem to bother him.

She moved into the kitchen and quietly began to make a pot of coffee. That was all she seemed to be good for. She couldn't find her son. She couldn't figure out who might have taken him. She didn't like feeling so useless, so utterly powerless. She'd had years of feeling that way with Frank and had sworn she'd never allow herself to feel that way again.

Only the first stir of dawn's light brightened the eastern skies and she turned on the small light over the oven, then poured herself a cup of the freshly brewed coffee.

As she sipped, she realized she was hungry, and that sent a stabbing guilt through her. How could she sleep? How could she even think about food when Billy had been kidnapped? Was he being fed? Was he warm? The questions tormented her.

"Good morning." Lucas's deep voice came from behind her and he flipped on the overhead light.

"It can't be good if Billy and Jenny aren't here," she replied.

She heard him open a cabinet and knew he was getting a cup for coffee. A minute later he joined her at the table. His sleep-tousled hair did nothing to detract from his handsomeness. She waited for him to tell her that he'd get them back, that everything was going to be okay. When he didn't, her heart clenched so tight she felt as if she were suffocating.

"At least we both got some sleep," he finally said.

She set her cup down. "I feel horrible, that I could sleep and not know if my son is being fed or being allowed to sleep. And you know what makes me feel even more guilty? The fact that at the moment I'm thinking about making some scrambled eggs and toast because I'm starving."

He reached across the table and captured her hand in his. "You can't feel guilty about the things your body requires to live. You have to eat and you have to sleep."

His hand was big and strong and warm around hers, and she welcomed the warmth, the touch. Maybe the old adage was true, that misery loved company.

"Are they coming home, Lucas?" The question was a mere whisper and until the words left her lips she hadn't realized she was going to ask it.

His gaze held hers. "I don't know." He squeezed her hand more tightly. "I wish I could tell you otherwise, but I don't think you'd appreciate me lying to you."

"Absolutely not," she agreed. "I want to know every piece of information you know, every feeling you have. I need to know what's going on every minute."

He nodded, released her hand and leaned back in his chair. "Now I have a very important question to ask you."

She sat up straighter, steeling herself for whatever he might need to know. "What?"

The corners of his lips turned up in a smile that momentarily erased the stress lines of his face. "Are you making the eggs or do you want me to? I have to confess I make a mean omelet."

Her burst of laughter surprised her, not only with its

unexpectedness but also in the fact that it eased some of the knot of tension in her stomach. She sobered almost immediately and pointed to the stove. "Knock yourself out. I don't think a man has ever cooked me breakfast before."

"Then sit back and relax and let me do the driving," he replied as he stood.

She watched as he began to pull items out of the refrigerator. "You like that, don't you? Being in the driver's seat."

He frowned thoughtfully as he set a carton of mushrooms on the counter. "I've never thought about whether I like it or not, it's just something I've always had to do."

"Why'd you decide to run for sheriff? It's no secret that you have enough money that if you didn't want to, you wouldn't have to work for the rest of your life."

He grabbed a knife from the drawer and began to cut up a green pepper. "When I was young I didn't know what I wanted to do with my life. There was a group of young men here in town. We were all friends and we spent most of our high school days acting like rich jackasses. We were overindulged, full of ourselves and good for nothing. Then the five of us decided to all go to the same college in Missouri."

He stopped talking long enough to get the skillet from the cabinet and the carton of eggs from the refrigerator, then continued. "Anyway, while we were there we all developed a social conscience. We called ourselves the Brotherhood and we all made a pact that we would choose careers that gave something back to our community. We were not going to be the kind of wealthy young men who got our names in the tabloids."

"So you became sheriff. What about the others in the Brotherhood?" She welcomed the conversation to keep her mind from dark places.

"You know Sawyer. He became an architect. Then there's Jackson Burdeaux, who is a criminal defense attorney, Clay Jefferson, who became a psychiatrist and Beau Reveneau, who joined the army."

"I've met all of them but Beau. Does he still live in Conja Creek?"

Lucas poured the egg concoction into the awaiting skillet before replying. "We don't know where Beau is. His family moved from Conja Creek about eight years ago, and none of us have heard from him for several years."

"So you were all close friends?"

"The best." He took a sip of his coffee, his expression reflective. "We swore that we'd always have each other's backs, that we'd support each other for the rest of our lives." He shook his head ruefully. "We were very young and idealistic."

"Must have been tough on you last month when you thought Sawyer had killed his wife," Mariah replied. The crime had been shocking. Sawyer's wife, Erica Bennett, had been stabbed and pushed off the dock and into the swamp water behind the Bennett home. Erica had been an unfaithful wife who at the time of her death had been pregnant. Sawyer had been the number-one suspect.

"The most difficult part was that I knew in my gut that Sawyer wasn't responsible, but I was pressured by your boss to make the arrest."

It had turned out that Erica had been murdered by

her best friend and next-door neighbor, Lillian Cordell. And despite all the drama, Sawyer had found love with the nanny he'd hired to care for his daughter, Molly.

"I hear Sawyer and Amanda are getting married next month," she said.

"Yeah. I got an invitation. It's going to be a small wedding in Sawyer's backyard. I'm glad he found somebody who makes him happy. He was unhappy with Erica for a very long time. And speaking of weddings and marriages, tell me about yours."

As always, whenever she thought of Frank, her wrist ached as if to remind her of all the pain her marriage had brought to her. "There's nothing much to tell. We got married, it didn't work out and we got a divorce."

"But there's more to it than that, isn't there?" He pushed the button to lower the bread in the toaster, then turned and looked at her expectantly.

"I'm surprised you'd find the minutia of a broken marriage of any interest," she replied.

"I think there's more than the usual minutia in your broken marriage. After all, it was you who told me Frank Landers might be responsible for all this."

As he took the eggs from the skillet and ladled them onto two plates, she turned her attention to the window and stared out, knowing that she was going to have to tell him how bad things had been, how stupid she had been. The toast popped up and she turned her gaze back to him.

"I was twenty-one and Frank was forty when we married. We'd met in a bar, and I thought he was strong and smart. He seemed to adore me."

She released a humorless laugh and wrapped her

hands around her coffee cup. "I guess you could say I was a cliché. My father left us when I was ten and I never had a real relationship with him. My mother worked two jobs to support us and I rarely saw her. When I met Frank I was hungry for somebody to love me, and he fed that hunger. It wasn't until after we were married that I realized his adoration was obsession and he was dictatorial and mean."

Lucas carried the two plates to the table and joined her there. She was grateful that his eyes held no judgment, nor did they hold pity. He just looked at her curiously.

"I was smart, but I fell into the same trap that other abused women fall into," she continued. "You've probably heard this story a million times before. At the beginning things were okay, although Frank had total control over what I did, where I went and who I saw. I wanted to please him so I played right into his game. By the time I got pregnant I'd been isolated from my friends and my mother. And while I knew things weren't right, I wanted my baby to be raised in the kind of complete family that I hadn't had."

"When did the physical abuse start?"

She looked at him in surprise. She hadn't mentioned anything about physical abuse. Unexpectedly, tears burned at her eyes as she thought of those years with Frank, years of fear and pain and broken dreams.

"About the time I got pregnant with Billy. Frank wasn't happy about the pregnancy, although initially I thought he'd come to embrace the idea of a child. The first time he laid a hand on me it was just a push...a shove. I fell into the coffee table and got banged up. He was instantly sorry and we put the incident behind us…until the next time."

"When did he hurt your wrist?"

She flushed and realized she'd been rubbing the ache since she'd begun talking about Frank. "The day I left him. By that time I'd been punched and kicked and slapped enough. I'd already begun to make plans to leave him, but that day he raised his hand to Billy. I stepped between them and he grabbed me by the wrist and twisted. I heard the snap when it broke. He drove me to the hospital, apologizing and telling me how much he loved me. But that snap of my wrist was a defining moment for me and I knew I wasn't leaving the hospital with him."

"You pressed charges?"

She nodded and once again wrapped her hands around her coffee cup, needing the warmth to infuse the chill that had taken up residence with the bad memories. "He spent a week in jail, then got out. Billy and I went into a shelter that night and we stayed at the shelter until the divorce was final. That day I packed up and Billy and I got into my car and left Shreveport and Frank Landers behind."

Lucas picked up his fork and pointed to her plate. "You'd better eat before it gets cold."

Although the hunger pangs that had gnawed at her had fled with the talk of Frank, she picked up her fork and took a bite. Instead of hunger, what gnawed at her now was a fire of simmering anger. She was angry with herself for falling into the trap of a battered woman, angry with Lucas for maintaining such control on his emotions, for fixing her eggs instead of finding her son.

She knew her emotions were irrational, that the anger she felt at the moment was misplaced, but she couldn't get a handle on it, and as she attempted to take another bite of her breakfast, it flared out of control.

"You remind me of him," she said.

He looked at her in surprise. "What are you talking about?"

"You remind me a lot of Frank." Careless abandon filled her. Her pain rose up inside her, so enormous she wanted to strike out and Lucas was a convenient target. "You treat Jenny a lot like Frank used to treat me."

He set his fork down and narrowed his dark eyes. "What does that mean? You're somehow comparing my relationship with my sister to the abusive relationship you had with your husband?"

"Oh, I'm sure you've never laid a hand on Jenny, but emotionally you do to her exactly what Frank used to do to me."

His narrowed eyes flickered with the heat of a burgeoning anger. "I think maybe your own emotional baggage is coloring the way you see things."

"On the contrary, my emotional baggage makes me see things more clearly." She wanted an explosion, needed to release not only the tension that balled so tight inside her, but also to diminish the physical attraction she felt for him.

What she wanted more than anything else was for him to reach out to her, to grab her and hold her tight in his arms as he had done the night before in the cemetery.

As crazy as it sounded, she wanted him to take her to bed, to fill her heart with anything other than the agonizing horror that was in there now. And that scared the hell out of her.

"You undermine her confidence, you belittle the choices she makes." She got up from the table, unable to sit next to him and say the things that threatened to burst from her. "You never let her forget that you have to rescue her, that she isn't smart enough, isn't old enough to do things right. That's abuse, Lucas, whether you recognize it or not, whether you mean it or not, it's abuse."

A muscle ticked in his jaw and his eyes were as dark as the night that had just passed. "You don't know what you're talking about. You don't know anything about me or my sister and the relationship we have."

"I know what I see. Did you know that Jenny wanted to be a teacher? But that's not what you wanted her to be. So she flunked out of college on purpose, because that's what you secretly expected of her, because she'd rather disappoint you than stand up to you." She took a step backward, somewhere in the back of her mind appalled at her audacity, yet unable to stop herself.

"You treat her like she's stupid and worthless and that's what she becomes when she's around you. You've stolen her self-esteem. Believe me, I know all about that." Tears fell down her cheeks and she swiped at them angrily.

"You have no idea what a great woman Jenny is. She would have made an awesome teacher, and my only consolation right now is that Jenny is with Billy wherever he is and I know she'll do everything in her power to keep him safe."

She left the kitchen then, horrified by her own

words and consumed with the emotion she'd tried so hard to control since the moment she'd realized Billy had been kidnapped.

LUCAS STARED AFTER HER, stunned first by her emotional outburst and secondly by what she'd said to him. As his surprise abated, anger welled up inside him.

Who in the hell did she think she was? How could she possibly compare him to an abuser? She knew nothing about him, nothing about Jenny.

Lucas pushed away from the table and stood, his intention to chase after her, but by the time he reached the living room he decided to give himself a few minutes to cool off.

He returned to the kitchen and cleaned up the dishes, his head whirling with his thoughts.

She was under an enormous amount of stress, he told himself. Surely she didn't really believe those things about him. He was not abusive to Jenny, he was just trying to save her from turning into the kind of woman who had given them birth.

Mariah didn't understand him, didn't understand where he was coming from where Jenny was concerned. And in any case he certainly didn't owe her any explanations or apologies for how he conducted himself with his sister.

He grabbed his overnight bag, his cell phone and a clean uniform and headed for the bathroom. Maybe beneath a refreshing cool shower some of his anger would dissipate.

It worked. As he stood beneath the spray of water he couldn't sustain the anger that had momentarily gripped him. Instead, a swell of sorrow filled him for her. He couldn't imagine being a young woman with a small child and having to run away in fear from the man who had promised to honor and cherish her.

He'd suspected secrets were in her past, and now she'd shared them with him. Was it any wonder she saw imagined abuse in others? She'd been through hell and had survived only to have her son ripped away from her by some unknown perpetrator.

Dammit. He wanted to be a hero for her. Her father had left her, her husband had abused her. She needed a hero. He wanted to bring her son home safe and sound. And he wanted to be a hero for Jenny. He leaned weakly against the shower wall as his head filled with thoughts of her.

He'd refused to allow himself to dwell on her, had instead tried to keep his focus on Billy. But now a rush of fear consumed him, clenching his stomach muscles as he broke into a cold sweat.

Jenny. His heart cried her name. From the time she'd been born, he'd taken care of her, seen to her needs and protected her from the world. And now he couldn't do any of those things. She was gone, taken for some reason he couldn't discern by a madman playing a game.

He hadn't cried when his mother died. He hadn't shed a tear when his wife had walked out on him, but the thought of never seeing his sister again pulled a deep sob from the very depths of him.

He sucked in a deep breath and stuffed his emotions deep inside. The only way he'd be able to get through this was to keep emotional distance. He wasn't just one of the victims' brother, he was the sheriff of Conja Creek and had to be strong, if not for himself, then for Mariah.

Getting out of the shower, he grabbed a towel and quickly dried off, then dressed in his clean clothes. He opened the bathroom door and bumped into Mariah, who had apparently been waiting for him.

"I'm sorry," she said, obviously tortured. "I was way out of line and I apologize. It's really none of my business."

"Apology accepted," he replied easily. There was nothing to gain by holding on to a grudge, and she obviously felt terrible about what had happened between them.

"I'm scared and I'm angry and you were convenient to vent to," she continued. She worried a hand through her hair. "I don't know why I said those things."

He held up a hand to halt anything else she might say. "We're under a lot of stress. As far as I'm concerned it's forgotten."

"I guess I'm just finding it difficult to think about facing another day," she said as he stepped out of the bathroom door and into the hallway.

"I know." He couldn't fight the impulse to draw her into his embrace. Despite the things she'd said to him, in spite of the fact that he should be angry with her, he felt her need to be held. Or was it his own need?

He pulled her against him, molding her curves against him as her arms wound around his neck. She was soft and warm and yielding.

She buried her face into the front of his shirt as her body trembled. He tightened his arms around her, wishing he could provide a barrier between her and her heartache.

He rubbed his hand down her back and tried to focus on giving comfort instead of the rising desire that filled him with her intimate nearness.

They stood that way for several long minutes, then she raised her head to look at him. He had no intention of kissing her, but as her full, sensual lips parted, he lowered his head and covered them with his own.

He half expected her to pull away, knew somehow that the kiss was out of line, crossing a boundary that shouldn't be crossed, but she didn't pull away. Instead, she seemed to move closer to him.

Her mouth opened to him and he deepened the kiss with his tongue as full-blown desire crashed through him. She returned the kiss, her tongue battling with his.

Her hands tangled in his hair at the nape of his neck and a slight moan escaped her, only increasing his need to take her.

Yet in the back of his mind he knew this was wrong. He felt as if he were taking advantage of her, exploiting her vulnerability. Reluctantly he broke the kiss.

She stared up at him and swallowed. "Temporary insanity," she said, her voice hoarse as she stepped back.

He was saved from making a reply by the ring of his cell phone. He listened to what his deputy had to tell him, then clicked off.

"That was Wally," he said to Mariah. "He picked up Remy Troulous and has him down at the office for questioning."

Her features lit with hope. "Surely he'll tell us if he knows anything about this. Just let me talk to him. I'm sure I can get him to tell us what he knows."

He didn't have the heart to tell her that Remy Troulous was a man who wouldn't be moved by a mother's pleas. If Remy didn't want to cooperate, there was nothing on this earth or beyond that would make him do so.

Chapter Seven

Mariah was grateful that he didn't mention the kiss as they drove to the sheriff's office. She couldn't imagine what had possessed her. But more, she couldn't imagine what had possessed him.

By all rights he should have been livid with her. She'd said terrible things to him, but her bad behavior certainly hadn't stopped him from kissing her.

Definitely temporary insanity, and it was obviously a state they had both suffered—for just a moment at the exact same time.

She was acutely conscious of him and she couldn't understand it. She wasn't even sure she liked him that well, but all she could think about was the heat of his mouth against hers, the memory of his hard body holding her tight.

How easy it was to focus on these things when the only other emotion she had inside her was wrenching, chilling fear. Her need for Lucas was so much simpler than all the other emotions that filled her at the moment.

"Did Wally say where he picked up Remy?" she

asked, finally breaking the uncomfortable silence that had ballooned between them.

"He didn't say, and with Remy it's hard to tell where Wally might have found him." Lucas turned onto Main Street.

The sun broke over the horizon, painting the buildings with a burst of gold light and dancing on the flowers that bloomed in pots in front of the shops.

Monday morning. She should be getting Billy out of bed and ready to go to the babysitter so she could go to work. She closed her eyes as she thought of sitting on the side of the bed next to her sleeping son. He always slept on his side, curled up in a warm toasty ball, and he always woke up with a smile.

He'd been a sunny child from the moment he'd been born. The only thing that had been able to put a cloud in his eyes had been his father.

She opened her eyes, consciously willing away the painful memories as Lucas pulled up in front of the sheriff's office. Please, she prayed. Please let the answer to where Jenny and Billy are rest with Remy Troulous. And please, let him talk to us.

Wally sat at the desk just inside the door and he rose as they entered. "Morning, Sheriff...Mariah." He nodded to them somberly. "I got him cooling his heels in the interview room. I'll warn you, he's not a happy camper."

Agent Michael Kessler also rose from the desk nearby. He walked over and introduced himself to Mariah. "Nice to meet you, although I'm sorry about the circumstances. I've been trying to run down your ex-husband," he said.

"No luck?"

Michael shook his head. "He hasn't registered a car in his name for the past two years nor can I find an employment record for him. I'll keep hunting, and in the meantime I've been interviewing locals for information." He gestured toward the interview room and looked at Lucas. "I'd like to be present when you interview Remy Troulous."

Lucas nodded, then looked at Mariah. "Initially, I want you to sit and watch outside of the room," Lucas said to her. "Let me and Agent Kessler have a go at him and see what happens."

"Before you do that, Louis got some information about Phillip Ribideaux you might find interesting," Wally said.

"And what's that?"

"It seems that ne'er-do-well Phillip has been cut off. According to his friends, his daddy got fed up with him and stopped the gravy train. Young Phillip now has to get a job and pay his own expenses."

Mariah watched the play of emotions on Lucas's face. He looked slightly dangerous, with a muscle ticking in his jaw and his dark-brown eyes narrowed. It was hard to believe that this was the same man who had minutes earlier held her so tenderly and kissed her with a fire that had momentarily chased away the arctic chill that had possessed her for the past two days.

"Louis is still sitting on him?"

Wally nodded. "But no offense, chief, somebody's going to have to take over for him so Louis can get some sleep."

"When Ed comes in this morning, put him on Ribideaux for the next twenty-four hours." Lucas looked at Mariah. "Maybe this is about a ransom after all.

Maybe Ribideaux got desperate when his father financially cut him off."

"Then why hasn't he made a ransom demand?" Mariah asked.

Lucas's eyes were dark as he held her gaze. "Right now the only answer I have is that whoever is holding Billy and Jenny is enjoying the game. Once the ransom demand is made, the game is over." He took her elbow and nodded to Agent Kessler. "Come on, let's go see what Remy Troulous has to add to this mix."

Lucas led her to a closet-size room with a window that looked into the next room. Inside the bigger area was a long conference table, and seated at the table was a handsome dark-haired young man.

He was sprawled in the chair with the arrogance of youth, legs up on the table and a smirk on his full, sensual lips. He wore a pair of worn jeans and a sleeveless shirt and had a large tattoo on his right shoulder. The tattoo was two letters—VP. Mariah guessed it stood for Voodoo Priests.

"I'll be right back," Lucas said as he gestured her to a chair.

She sat and stared at the young man, wondering if he had entered her home and somehow tricked Billy and Jenny into going with him, or forced them from the house at gunpoint. Or perhaps he'd encountered them in the park and seen an opportunity.

Although he looked like a punk, he didn't look evil. She had to remind herself that evil often wore a benign face. True evil could hide behind an easy smile and laughing eyes.

She drew a deep, tremulous breath and stared at the

man in front of her. Did the answer to Billy and Jenny's whereabouts rest with Remy Troulous?

She moved to the edge of the chair as she saw Lucas and Agent Kessler enter the interview room. "Get your feet off the table," Lucas said to Remy. "You might do that at your house, but you're in my house now."

For a moment Remy didn't move. He stared up at Lucas with insolent challenge, and Mariah could feel the tension between the two even though she wasn't in the same room.

She released a small sigh as Remy pulled his feet from the table and sat up straighter in the chair. "Why is it that whenever anything goes wrong in this town one of your men hauls me down here?" Remy asked.

"Because when things go wrong, you're usually in the middle of them." Lucas remained standing. He looked fierce, like a warrior facing his enemy. "You know my sister is missing?" Kessler stood just inside the door, obviously not intending to be an active participant in the questioning.

Remy laughed. "This is a small town, Sheriff. Somebody coughs in one house and the next-door neighbor calls somebody else to tell about it. Nothing much happens here that everyone doesn't know about."

Mariah studied Remy's face, watching his handsome features for signs of something, anything that would indicate he was behind the kidnapping.

"I don't know why your deputy dragged me down here," Remy continued. "I don't know anything about your sister's disappearance."

"One of her friends told me she'd been seeing you." Lucas took a step closer to where Remy sat.

"That's crazy," Remy exclaimed as he broke eye contact with Lucas. "What would somebody like me be doing with the sheriff's sister? Get real, why don't you?"

"Where were you on Friday between the hours of ten and five?"

Remy laughed once again, the sound deep and pleasant. "I'm not sure where I was last night. I sure as hell don't remember where I was on Friday."

Lucas sat in the chair next to Remy. "I think maybe you need to try harder to remember."

Remy frowned and rubbed a hand across his forehead. "I don't know, I was probably hanging out with my boys, that's what I do most days. You can check with one of them, they'll vouch for me."

"You mean they'll lie for you," Lucas replied. "When was the last time you saw Jenny?"

"I don't know. I might have passed her on the street last week sometime. I got me a girl, Sheriff, I'm not interested in Jenny like that."

"Then why was she seeing you?" Lucas pressed. "What interest did you have in her?"

Remy's eyes narrowed and he blinked several times. "I told you already I wasn't seeing your sister, and that's all I got to say on the matter." He crossed his arms over his chest. "I don't know where your sister and that little boy are. I don't have anything to do with them being missing. And unless you're going to charge me with something, I'm leaving. Are you arresting me?"

Lucas shook his head. "Not at this time."

"Then I'm out of here," Remy replied.

Panic shot through Mariah as Remy stood. He was

their best lead, and if he walked out, who knew if and when they would get the opportunity to question him again.

Remy headed for the door and Lucas followed him with Agent Kessler trailing behind. Mariah jumped up from her chair and met them in the hallway.

"Mr. Troulous," she said. "I'm Mariah Harrington and it's my little boy who is missing with Jenny." She grabbed his hand and tried to ignore the smell that emanated from him, the odors of stale sweat and cheap beer and swamp. "Please, if you know anything that might help us find them, if you had anything to do with it, please tell me."

She held his hand tightly, as if it were a rope that held her dangling over an abyss of grief. If she released him, if he walked away, then she was afraid she'd fall and crash into a million pieces.

Remy looked distinctly uncomfortable as he tried to pull his hand from her grasp, but she held on, refusing to allow him to move away from her.

"Billy, that's my son. He has asthma and if he gets scared or stressed out he'll have an attack. He's a smart boy and he loves school and learning about new things. He loves to play baseball and he doesn't like the dark. He needs his medicine but more than anything he needs to be home with me. I need him home with me." A sob welled up in her throat.

"Look, lady. I'm sorry for your troubles, but I don't know anything about it." Remy looked at Lucas for help.

Lucas stepped closer and placed a hand on Mariah's shoulder. "Let him go, Mariah," he said gently.

She didn't want to let him go. She wanted to hold his hand until he confessed he'd kidnapped Jenny and Billy. She wanted to cling to him until he told them where he had the two stashed and how she and Lucas could bring them home safely. But his dark, heavy-lidded eyes let her know she could squeeze his hand through eternity and he wasn't going to give her the answers she needed.

Reluctantly she let go and dropped her hand to her side. Remy raced for the exit as Lucas took Mariah by the arm and led her out of the hallway and into the interview room, Kessler following just behind them.

Lucas pulled out a chair and motioned her to sit, as if aware that her trembling legs threatened to give out beneath her. Once she was seated, he left the room then returned with a bottle of water and set it in front of her.

She smiled at him gratefully and uncapped the bottle and took a drink. "You okay?" he asked as he perched on the table next to her chair.

She shrugged. "I guess I was expecting a Perry Mason moment. You know, you lean on him and he breaks and tells us everything we need to know. Stupid, huh."

"Not stupid," he protested. "Just maybe a bit naive."

"I'll tell you what was smart on your part. Talking about Billy like you did," Agent Kessler said.

"What do you mean?" She looked at the blond-haired man curiously.

"You said his name, told Remy a little bit about him. You personalized Billy to the man you thought might have him. That's a smart thing to do. It's what hostage negotiators do when they're trying to resolve a situation."

She sighed wearily. "I don't understand how two people could seemingly disappear from the face of the earth and nobody knows what happened." She put the cap back on the bottle of water and fought against the wave of overwhelming despair that threatened to consume her.

"Why don't you just hang tight right here," Lucas said. "We need to coordinate with my men." He stood. "You need anything?"

"The only thing I need is the one thing nobody seems to be able to get for me," she replied.

They left her then, alone in the interview room with only her faltering hope to keep her company.

THE MEN WERE ALL THERE except Ed, who had taken over sitting on Phillip Ribideaux for Louis. It took almost an hour for them to exchange pertinent information. Wally had been in touch with the phone company, trying to trace the calls that had gone to both Lucas's cell phone and Mariah's home number. As Lucas had suspected, other than the call that had come from the pay phone, the calls had been made by disposable cell phones that were almost impossible to trace.

He'd given the original copies of the recorded messages to Kessler, who would forward them to specialists in the hopes that they could identify a background noise or a voice pattern that might lead to a suspect.

Louis added that while he'd had Phillip Ribideaux under surveillance, the young man hadn't gone anywhere or done anything suspicious. After losing him, Louis had picked up his trail again at his house, where Phillip and some of his friends had spent most of the night drinking beer and packing a rental moving van.

Ben had searched the cemetery to look for the bullet, but hadn't found it.

There was still no word from Shreveport about Frank Landers and no other potential suspects on the list. Lucas instructed Ben to grab a couple of citizens who'd volunteered their time, and search all the empty buildings and storefronts in the city.

With nothing more to do, Lucas left his men and headed back to the interview room. Before he reached it, on impulse he went into the smaller room, sat in the chair and gazed at Mariah through the one-sided glass.

She sat with her profile to him, staring at the wall with no expression on her face. Her shoulders were rigidly straight and she seemed to scarcely be breathing.

He thought of the things she'd said to him during breakfast. Did he really remind her of her abusive ex-husband? Was he too overbearing with Jenny? In his concern that she not become a woman like their mother, had he stolen his sister's self-esteem?

Jenny had once mentioned that she'd like to be a teacher, but he had been adamant that a business degree was a smarter decision. He had just been trying to steer her in the right direction. Was that abusive?

Irritated with his thoughts and with the small flutter of self-doubt that suddenly assailed him, he stood. Dammit, he had more important things to be concerned with than analyzing his relationship with Jenny. He had to *find* her.

He got up from the chair and went into the interview room. Mariah stood as he entered, looking weary despite it being just noon.

"Let's get you home," he said.

She nodded and together they left the office and headed back to her house. They didn't speak. It was as if the failure to learn anything from Remy sat between them, creating a barrier too big for words to get around.

The minute they were back in her kitchen, they both saw the blinking message light. Lucas checked the information on the recorder. One recorded message, and it had come in three minutes before they'd walked through the front door. Without even playing it, he knew it was from the kidnapper.

Mariah grabbed one of his hands as he punched the button and the now-familiar voice filled the kitchen. "No answers at the office, right? Well, I have a little something for you. By the twisted tree you'll find a clue, where the grass is green and the sky is blue. Where the flowers bloom you'll find something rare. So go there now if you think you dare."

Lucas wanted to punch something. The bastard was watching their every move. He seemed to know what they were doing almost before they did it.

"It's the park," Mariah said, her blue eyes lighting with life. "A twisted tree, I know the tree. It's near the swings in the park."

Lucas frowned. "There must be a hundred twisted trees in Conja Creek."

Her eyes flashed with a touch of impatience. "But he would pick the one we know. Everyone refers to the tree in the park as the twisted tree. It's got to be the one in the park."

Mariah's excitement was contagious, but Lucas tried not to get his hopes up. He hated the bright shine of optimism that shone in her eyes—a shine that could so easily be doused.

"Mariah," he began cautiously. "We thought we were going to get something positive when we went to the cemetery, but the only thing we got was shot at."

"Surely he wouldn't do that again." She headed for the front door. "He says there's a clue there. He didn't say that about the cemetery. This is different. I couldn't live with myself if I didn't check it out." The words bubbled out of her, as if escaping an intense internal pressure. "Maybe this time he'll give us something to go on, or at least something to let us know that Jenny and Billy are still okay."

Lucas hurried after her and a moment later he backed out of her driveway and headed for the nearby neighborhood park. He had a bad feeling about this. It worried him that the caller had known that they'd been at the sheriff's office. It enraged him that the kidnapper was obviously close enough to them to know what they were doing and when they were doing it.

Who in the hell was behind this? It was possible Remy had made the call the moment he'd left the office. He probably possessed more than one cell phone that could be used to make the anonymous calls.

Lucas believed Remy hadn't been completely forthcoming, especially when Lucas had questioned him about why he'd been seeing Jenny. Although Remy had professed that he wasn't seeing Lucas's sister, Lucas hadn't believed him. Remy had avoided his glance when he'd answered and blinked one too many times, like liars usually did.

It bothered him that a ransom demand hadn't been made. That meant this was about something more than money. That meant it was something personal. And with both Jenny and Billy taken, it was impossible to know who was the real target.

The park was empty when they arrived, probably due to the intense heat and humidity of the day. Mariah was out of the car almost before Lucas had brought it to a complete halt. She raced across the parking lot toward the gnarled tree that rose up near the swing set. He ran after her, his hand on the butt of his gun.

"Mariah, wait," he called. Dammit, he didn't know if they were walking into some sort of a trap again or not. She didn't slow down.

He caught up with her when she halted in front of the tree. He grabbed her by the arm and pulled her to the ground. "What are you doing?" she asked.

"Have you forgotten what happened the last time we followed the caller's clue? Just stay down for a minute and let me assess things." He held on to her arm with one hand and kept his other on his gun.

He gazed around the area, not liking that the south side of the park was flanked by a wooded area that provided plenty of cover if somebody wanted to hide there.

"Lucas, if he wanted to kill us, we'd be dead," Mariah said softly. "If we're dead, the game ends and we both know that doesn't seem to be what the kidnapper wants."

As much as he hated to admit it, she made sense. The

kidnapper was obviously getting off on running them around town, feeding their fear and anxiety. If he killed one or both of them, his game would be over.

Mariah stood and began to search the tree. She looked up into the branches, then walked around it, checking out the trunk. Lucas looked as well, but found nothing. "'Where the flowers bloom you'll find something rare,'" Mariah said, and her gaze focused on the flower bed in the distance. "It's not the tree, it's the flower bed," she exclaimed.

A deep weariness overtook Lucas. "Let's see if he really left us something or if this is just another step in his sick game."

Chapter Eight

Mariah raced toward the flower bed, her heart pounding with the rhythm of hope…of fear…and a million other emotions. Surely he wouldn't send them out for nothing again. Nobody could be that cruel.

There had to be something here, something that would feed the small glimmer of hope that still existed in her heart. As each hour passed, in the deepest, darkest places inside her, hope was becoming more and more difficult to sustain.

She'd somehow believed that if Billy were dead she'd know it in her heart, in her soul. But over the past couple of days she'd realized that wasn't true. It was possible Billy and Jenny had been murdered in the first hours of their disappearance, and she hadn't felt the loss.

As she stared at the flower bed, she refused to consider that scenario. They had to still be alive. Any other possibility was too horrific to contemplate.

"It doesn't look like any of the flowers have been disturbed," Lucas said as he stood next to her.

"There's got to be something here," she replied. She

stepped into the flower bed and sank to her hands and knees and began to pull at the flowers to see if any of them had been uprooted, then just set back in the ground.

A note, a piece of fabric, something, there had to be something buried beneath the flowers. That's what the caller had implied. It was a treasure hunt and she was desperate to find the treasure.

She pulled and tugged, more frantic with each minute that passed. It had to be here. Something had to be here. She couldn't come away from here without anything and continue to maintain her sanity.

She scrambled at the dirt, unmindful of the flowers she destroyed in her efforts. Flowers could be replaced, but Billy couldn't. Jenny couldn't.

A clawing, frantic desperation built inside her as she dug in the hard dirt with her fingers. She ignored Lucas, who stood just behind her. He wasn't digging, and she knew it was because he didn't believe anything was here. But she had to believe.

"Mariah, there's nothing here." Lucas's voice was flat, without emotion.

She ignored him, moving to a new place in the flower bed. Her fingers hurt from the contact with the hard earth, but she ignored the pain, scrabbling against the ground, uprooting flowers as her breaths came in frantic gasps. She felt half-demented with her need.

"Mariah, you need to stop." Lucas's voice seemed to come from very far away.

"No. Something's here. I know it is." She continued to dig, tears starting to blur her vision. She needed to find it. The clue. The caller had said there was a clue.

"Mariah." Lucas grabbed one of her arms. She jerked away from him, moving to yet another area and continuing her search. Tears became sobs as she dug.

Lucas grabbed her once again, this time more forcefully. "Mariah, dammit, stop. You have to stop! There's nothing here. He's yanking our chain."

As Lucas pulled her to her feet she fought him, slamming her fists into his chest as deep, wrenching sobs exploded from her.

"Let me go," she cried, mindless with anger, with a new kind of grief. "I have to find it."

"There's nothing here to find," he exclaimed, and he pulled her tight against him, holding her so she couldn't move, couldn't escape.

Somewhere in the back of her mind she knew he was right, that there was nothing to find, no clue that would magically lead to Billy. She quit fighting him and instead leaned weakly against him, sobbing as she broke completely.

He held her tight, rubbing her back as she clung to him. "Shh, I know," he whispered.

She cried harder, tears that had been trapped deep inside her since the first night of the disappearance.

"I'm sorry," he whispered. "Let it out. Just let it all out."

Her tears weren't just for herself and her son, but also for him and his sister. And she knew he understood better than anyone the utter despair she felt. Surely he felt the same bitter disappointment that she did. They were no closer to finding Jenny than they were to finding Billy.

They stood in the embrace for a long time as slowly,

painfully, Mariah cried herself out. When her tears were finally gone, there was nothing left inside her.

She was depleted...of emotion, of life. First the interview with Remy and now this, all for nothing. She was completely empty, numb.

"Come on, let's get you home," Lucas said gently.

Home, she thought. That place wasn't a home. Not with Billy gone.

He led her to his car, and she slid into the passenger seat. She'd never felt so numb, as if she were dead. She closed her eyes and only opened them again when the car stopped in her driveway.

She stared at the house that she'd thought would be the place she and Billy would find happiness. They were finally free of Frank, and she'd been filled with such hope when she'd rented the house.

She'd hoped that Conja Creek would be the place where she could work a decent job and raise Billy with the kind of stability and joy that had been missing in the first years of his life.

She'd believed the biggest threat in her life was Frank, and when she'd finally escaped his grasp she thought it would be smooth sailing. She'd been a fool to expect happiness. She'd been a fool to believe that such a state of being was even possible for her.

"Come on," Lucas said, pulling her from her thoughts. "You need a hot shower, and we need to do something about your hands."

She looked at her hands, surprised to see that her knuckles were cut and bloody and her nails were chipped and torn.

Wearily she got out of the car, the numbness slowly passing as a chill took over. Lucas wrapped an arm around her shoulder as they entered the house, and by the time he led her to the bathroom she was trembling uncontrollably.

He started the water in the shower and laid out a clean towel for her. "After you get out, we'll attend to those hands." He stepped out of the bathroom and closed the door behind him.

She slowly undressed and got beneath the hot spray of water, leaning weakly against the wall. She'd never felt so empty inside, as if everything that made her a living, breathing person had been drained away.

It scared her, the utter void. Even during the worst of times with Frank she'd never felt this way. Billy, her heart cried. Where are you?

She got out of the shower and dried off. She pulled a brush through her hair, then put on the white terry-cloth robe she retrieved from the hook on the back of the bathroom door.

Throwing her dirty clothes into her hamper, she felt lost. When she opened the bathroom door, she saw Lucas leaning against the wall in the hall and she knew in that instant what she needed, what she wanted. She needed some temporary insanity and she knew exactly who could give it to her.

LUCAS SIGHED IN RELIEF as she stepped out of the bathroom. She'd scared him. As she'd frantically dug in the flower bed, she'd been like a demented woman, and he was afraid she'd snapped.

But wrapped in a white robe, smelling like minty soap

and with her hair damp, she appeared to be back in control. The crazy, zealous light in her eyes was gone.

"Better?" he asked.

To his surprise she stepped up directly in front of him, so close he could feel her soft breath on his face. "No, I'm not better." Her blue eyes shimmered as she gazed up at him. "I'm cold inside and empty and I need you to make me warm. I need you to make me feel alive again." She wrapped her arms around his neck.

He stiffened and kept his hands at his sides, fighting the impulse to wrap her in his arms and pull her tightly, intimately against him. "Mariah, you're in a bad place right now. We don't want to do anything we'll regret later."

She pressed closer to him, and the first stir of desire didn't just simmer inside him, it crashed through him.

"No regrets," she replied. "I need you, Lucas. I need you to take me in your arms and make love to me. I need to make myself forget everything for just a little while." Her voice trembled slightly.

"Mariah, I don't want to take advantage of you," he replied. He held himself rigid and tried not to think about her naked beneath the robe.

"You aren't. I'm taking advantage of you." She rose up on tiptoe and placed her lips against the underside of his jaw.

Lucas closed his eyes, fighting to be strong. But her lips were hot and sensual against his neck, and as she moved her hips against his the control he'd fought to maintain the last couple of days snapped.

He took her mouth with his, losing himself in the hunger for her and the momentary respite from the horror that had become her life and his own.

The kiss lasted only a moment, then she broke it, took his hand and led him down the hall to her bedroom. There was no hesitation in her step, and her hand held tight to his, as if she was afraid he might try to break away and run.

When they reached her bedroom, she dropped his hand and began to unbutton his shirt. As she worked the buttons, he unfastened his holster, took it off and set it on the nightstand.

Somewhere in the back of his mind he knew this was crazy, that there was no way making love to Mariah would make anything better, easier. It would probably make things worse. When this was all over she'd probably hate herself. But at the moment her need radiated from her and he also couldn't deny that he wanted her.

When his shirt was unbuttoned, she ripped it from his shoulders and tossed it to the floor, then she walked over to the bed, pulled down the scarlet spread and shrugged out of her robe. She stood before him naked.

His breath caught in his throat. With the sunshine streaming through the window, painting her skin in gold tones, she was achingly beautiful. As he fumbled to get out of his slacks, she slid into bed beneath the sheets.

Crazy. He knew they both had gone stark-raving crazy, but he gave in to it, refusing to allow doubts any room in his head. He placed his wallet on the nightstand, then, as naked as she, he got into the bed and pulled her into his arms.

There was a frantic desperation in the kiss they shared, and her naked skin against his drove him half-mad with desire. She was warm and sweetly scented and it had been a very long time since he'd been with a woman. Work and Jenny had kept him busy, and it had been over a year since he'd taken time for even a super-ficial personal relationship.

But it wasn't just that he was overdue for sexual release that had him gasping with want. It was Mariah herself.

She'd been nothing more than the mayor's secretary when this all began, but in the past couple of days Lucas had seen her interminable strength, and she'd shared with him her past heartaches. He admired her and he liked her, and that as much as anything fed his desire for her and only her.

Their lips remained locked as his hands cupped her full breasts. Her nipples sprang to attention at his touch, and he grazed his thumb over them as she uttered a soft moan.

He broke the kiss and instead nipped lightly at the side of her slender neck, down across her collarbone, then he captured one of her erect nipples in his mouth.

She wound her fingers into his hair as he licked and sucked. She arched to meet his hardness, but he wasn't ready to take her yet. He wanted her mindless with pleasure, knew that's what she wanted…to be mindless.

He ran his hand down the flat of her stomach, down across her hip bones and touched her intimately. She gasped and at the same time she grabbed him. Her hand was warm around him, and he drew a deep breath to steady himself, not wanting to rush things.

He moved his fingers against her, and her breathing quickened as her entire body tensed. Once again he covered her mouth with his as he felt her getting closer to her release.

She whispered his name and he nearly lost it and at the same time she arched and cried out with complete pleasure.

"Take me," she said with a thrumming urgency that radiated through him. "Please, Lucas. Now, please take me now."

He rolled off her and grabbed his wallet, fumbling for the condom he carried inside. It took him only a moment to get it out and on, then he positioned himself above her and gazed down into her eyes.

"It's not too late to stop," he said, his voice hoarse and ragged. "You can stop this right now if you want to. I won't be mad."

She reached up and placed her hand on his cheek, her eyes filled with a depth of emotion. "Don't stop," she said.

He entered her, sliding into her awaiting warmth with a slow, sure stroke. She moaned her pleasure and wrapped her arms around his back.

Slowly he moved against her, but it didn't take long before his own frantic need moved him faster and faster. She wasn't a passive lover. Her hands raked him as she threw her head back and gave herself completely to the act.

All too quickly he felt the build up, and just before he exploded, she cried his name and his release washed through him with an intensity he'd never known. He kissed her then, a soft, tender kiss.

He rolled to one side of her and she turned to face him. For a long moment her gaze remained locked with his, and in the depth of her eyes he saw her heartbreak once again darkening her eyes.

He stroked her face, a sense of failure sweeping through him. He might have taken her away for a few minutes, but until he brought her son home safe and sound, her pain wouldn't ever let her go.

And with each hour that passed, the possibility of bringing Billy home safe and sound grew dimmer.

BILLY WAS IN TROUBLE.

Jenny stared at the sleeping little boy and feared that he wouldn't make it through another night. The sound of his ragged breaths filled her with a fear she'd never known. He hadn't even had the energy to get off the mattress during the day.

He'd spent most of the time just lying there, the mere act of drawing breath taking every ounce of his strength. He didn't even have the strength to be afraid. He seemed resigned to whatever was going to happen, and Jenny wanted to weep because an eight-year-old boy shouldn't be resigned to his own death.

She walked around the small room and wondered if they both would die here. She didn't care so much about herself, but it wasn't fair that a little boy die in this ugly place without his mommy to hold him, to comfort him.

If she could just find a way out, or some means to summon help. But she'd been over the small room a hundred times and couldn't find a way to do either. She'd pulled at the boards that imprisoned them, seeking a weakness, a flaw in their prison, but there was none.

She'd just sunk to the floor when she heard the

sound. *A boat.* A motorboat. Maybe it was help! A search party. She sprang to her feet, hope raging through her. Maybe Lucas had found them!

Or maybe it was their kidnapper returning. The hope that had momentarily surged through her transformed to fear. She stood perfectly still, frozen as the sound of the boat grew closer…closer…then finally stopped.

There was a moment of complete silence, then heavy footsteps rang against wood. Jenny stifled a scream. If it were help, then somebody would have yelled. Somebody would have shouted their names.

The footsteps drew closer, then a slat in the door opened. Jenny ran to the door. "Hey…hey, you've got to get us out of here! He's sick. Billy has asthma and he's in bad trouble."

Dark eyes peered back at her, then the slat closed.

She slammed her fists against the door as she heard footsteps going away. "Wait, please come back. Did you hear what I said? He's in bad trouble. He needs to get to a hospital." Again and again she slammed her fists against the wood as she began to cry. "Don't go. For God's sake don't leave him here."

It was only when she heard the motor on the boat start up again that she stopped beating the door and sank to the floor in tears.

He was leaving. He was leaving them here. Tears blinded her and she fought against the deep sobs that welled inside her.

She turned and saw Billy watching her. She quickly swiped at her cheeks. She didn't want to cry in front of him. She didn't want to upset him any more than he already was.

"Hey, buddy." She scooted over next to him and pulled him into her arms. His wheezing seemed to intensify. She needed to distract him.

"Have I ever told you that female alligators usually lay about fifty eggs? Can you imagine having fifty kids?" As she told him everything she'd ever known about alligators and crocodiles, she felt him begin to relax against her.

But she couldn't relax for, more than fear of her own safety, her biggest fear was that when morning came, Billy would no longer be breathing.

Chapter Nine

Mariah awoke as the faint purple spill of dusk filtered through the window. The bed next to her was empty, but the pillow still retained the scent of Lucas's cologne.

She didn't feel guilty about making love with him. She didn't feel guilty about seeking warmth and life when her heart had been so dead. Nor did she have any illusions about what their lovemaking had meant. It had meant absolutely nothing.

Rolling over on her back, she stared up at the ceiling and realized that in some way the lovemaking and the sleep afterward had given her a new strength to survive whatever the rest of the evening might bring.

She got out of bed and dressed in a comfortable pair of gray jogging pants and a T-shirt, then went in search of Lucas. As she reached the hallway, she heard the voice of the kidnapper.

"...by the twisted tree you'll find a clue." She froze, heart banging against her rib cage.

The voice stopped, then started again. "...by the twisted tree you'll find a clue."

She relaxed a bit as she realized it wasn't a new call.

She followed the sound to the kitchen, where Lucas sat in front of the recording machine with a legal pad in front of him.

She stood in the doorway and watched as he pushed the Play button again. "Where the grass is green and the sky is blue." He punched the Stop button, then rubbed the center of his forehead with two fingers as he stared down at the legal pad.

"What are you doing?"

He looked up at the sound of her voice, then leaned back in his chair and sighed. "Making notes, listening to the messages, trying to make sense of all this."

She slid into the chair next to him. "And have you managed to make any sense of it?"

He shook his head. "No." He leaned back in the chair and released a weary sigh. "I'll tell you what we know. There was no sign of forced entry, so the odds are good that Jenny knew the kidnapper, that she not only knew him but trusted him enough to open the door to him. If they were taken from here."

She frowned. "What do you mean? Of course they were taken from here."

"We don't know that for sure. We don't really know where the crime scene is located. For all we know they were taken from the front yard or the park."

She frowned. He had mentioned that before, but she couldn't imagine Jenny and Billy being hustled into a car off the street or taken from the park...unless they knew their kidnapper...unless they'd trusted the kidnapper. That thought certainly didn't make her feel any better.

He flipped through his legal pad. "We also know that

the kidnapper is watching us. He was in the cemetery the other night, and he knew that we'd gone to the sheriff's office this morning. Something else that strikes me is that he doesn't seem to want dialogue, but instead wants monologues."

She frowned at him curiously. "What do you mean?"

He leaned forward. "Other than the first call that I got and the one that Wally answered, he hasn't called to talk to us, but rather to leave messages on the machine. He's specifically chosen times when he knows we aren't here. He wants to talk to us, but he doesn't want us talking to him."

"So what would happen if we don't leave here? If we answer every call that comes in instead of letting the machine pick up. Would he stop calling?"

"It would be interesting to see," he replied.

A flash of anger burned inside her. "He might think he's playing a game with us, but he's not. Games have rules and when he says there's a clue, then there should be a clue." She released a bitter laugh. "I know it's ridiculous for me to be mad because a kidnapper doesn't play by the rules I think are fair."

Lucas nodded, his forehead still furrowed with a frown. "Our two main suspects are Remy Troulous and Phillip Ribideaux. I know Phillip has been financially cut off by his father."

"Which might make him desperate enough to kidnap for a ransom," she said. "He certainly doesn't have the tools to make a living the right way."

"But…I keep going back to the same problem. If this is about a ransom, then why take Billy?"

"Because he saw the kidnapper?"

He nodded. "Then we have Frank Landers, whom we can't locate and have no idea if he has a hand in this. And if he took Billy, then why Jenny?"

"For the same reason. Because she saw him and could identify him."

"I feel like we're going in circles," he said in frustration. He swiped a hand through his dark hair, and for a moment she remembered what those dark, rich strands had felt like between her fingers.

"Let's take the suspects one at a time," she said, focusing on the conversation. "We can pinpoint a plausible motive for Phillip. Maybe he's just entertaining himself before making a ransom demand. What about Remy? Same motive? Money?"

Lucas sighed again. "The longer this thing goes on, the less I think it's about money."

"What other motive could Phillip have?" she asked.

"Who knows? I know Jenny was talking a lot of smack about him after they broke up. Maybe he's trying to teach her a lesson."

"And what about Remy? If you take away a money motive, then why would he be involved in something like this?" It helped, talking rationally about all the players. It felt constructive, and that was what she needed at the moment.

"Who knows what drives Remy? Certainly he's always walked a line outside the law. I don't think he was forthcoming in his answers to me about seeing Jenny, but I can't imagine what he hopes to gain by a kidnapping."

"It could be Frank," Mariah said. "The caller is getting off on tormenting us. That's definitely Frank's style."

Lucas reached out and covered her hand with his. "I'm sorry you had to go through what you did with him."

The warmth of his hand was welcome, and she offered him a small smile. "I survived. But, as sheriff of this parish, you should know that if I find out he's responsible for this, I might just kill him."

"I understand the sentiment," he replied, and by the darkness in his eyes she knew he felt the same rage that she did.

She pulled her hand from his and leaned back in her chair. "Any other viable suspects?"

"No, and that's what's so damned frustrating. Not knowing for sure what the motive might be makes pointing a finger at a viable suspect that much more difficult." He tapped the recorder. "And what's driving me crazy is that there's something about the caller's voice that's vaguely familiar, but I can't figure out what it is."

This time it was her turn to place her hand over his. "You're doing everything you can. You've got people searching and watching the suspects. There's only so much you can do with so little to go on."

He smiled, filling her with a welcome warmth. "I'm the one who's supposed to be making you feel better."

"Then who makes *you* feel better? Why have you remained alone?" During the past couple of days she'd seen a side of Lucas she'd never guessed he would have possessed. It was a tender and gentle side that was in direct contrast to the kind of man she'd believed him to be.

He rose from the table and went to the counter,

where the pot of coffee was still warm. He poured himself a cup. "Want one?"

She shook her head, and he returned to the table.

"When my wife left me I decided to devote my life to Jenny. Someplace in the back of my mind, I knew that women would come and go, but that my sister would always need me. She had nobody else. I have my work and I date occasionally, and for the most part that's been enough for me."

"But a sister and work can't be a partner for life," she replied.

He cast her a wry smile. "Jenny could definitely be a job for life."

She bit her tongue, not wanting to begin another contentious discussion about his relationship with his sister.

He seemed to read her mind. "You have to understand where we came from. My old man died when Jenny was just a baby and our mother, who was never real maternal, seemed to forget she was a parent."

He got up from the table as if unable to sit any longer and began to pace the small confines of the room. "Mom was one of those women who thrived on attention and drama. She wasn't happy unless everything was in an uproar, and she definitely wasn't happy if she wasn't with a man." He paused and stared at the wall just over her head, his eyes dark with memories.

He focused back on Mariah. "Maybe I have been too hard on Jenny. I've just been so afraid she'd turn out like our mother. Mom killed herself with drugs. I don't think she meant to die, but she had just broken up with some loser and I think the suicide was an attempt to get him back. She took pills then called him, but he didn't believe her and she died."

"But you've accomplished what you wanted. Jenny is nothing like the woman you've described," Mariah said softly. Certainly what he'd just told her helped in her understanding of his relationship with Jenny.

He stared at her for a long moment. "If I've been the man you described, if I've been emotionally abusive and overbearing to her, my biggest fear now is that I won't get the chance to change things."

His voice broke and Mariah rose from her chair and walked to where he stood. She wrapped her arms tightly around him, knowing the torment that was in his heart.

"You'll get your chance to make things right with Jenny," she said. "And I'm going to get the chance to see my son grow up." She said the words fervently, but what frightened her more than anything was she wasn't sure she believed them anymore.

Lucas stood at the front window, staring into the bright afternoon sunshine. He stretched, attempting to unkink muscles that had been knotted from the moment he'd awakened on the sofa that morning.

He'd spent a miserable night with horrible dreams of Jenny crying out to him and him unable to find her. When Mariah had gotten up, it had been obvious that she'd spent an equally miserable night. Her face had been lined with stress, and exhaustion had placed even darker circles under her eyes.

He wanted to be outside, searching, but he'd determined that the best place for him to be was here, waiting for another phone call. This time the caller wouldn't talk to a machine, but to him.

Mariah had gone back to her bedroom a little while ago, and Lucas had almost been grateful that she had. Their conversation had been empty and strained today, as if the emotional outbursts from the day before had drained all the energy, all the will from them both.

Enough time had passed, now, that most of the concerned citizens who had come out on that first day to help search would have returned to their jobs, their lives.

Even when a young woman and a little boy were missing, life went on. What if they never found Jenny and Billy? People disappeared every day, and when foul play was involved bodies were often never found.

How would Mariah cope if Billy never came home? She'd survive, because she was a survivor, but her life would never be the same. He felt confident that she wouldn't remain in Conja Creek, that the town itself and this house in particular would hold too many bad memories for her to stay.

He would miss her. The thought shocked him. In the course of these past days, he'd grown closer to her than he could ever have imagined, closer than he'd been to anyone for a very long time. He felt he knew her better than anyone, but more than that, he felt she knew him.

Lucas recognized he could fall for her if he allowed himself. But he wouldn't allow it, because even though she'd made love with him, he guessed that the emotions they felt were driven by circumstance.

Sooner or later this case would be resolved one way or another, and with that resolution would come an end to the unusual and intense relationship they'd forged.

As he moved away from the window, he realized it was time for him to build a wall around his emotions where she was concerned. He'd allowed himself to get too close, both in his position as sheriff and as a man.

He returned to the kitchen, where his legal pad awaited him at the table. One thing he and Mariah hadn't discussed the day before when they'd been going over things was the fact that the kidnapper could be almost anyone.

Just because they had Phillip Ribideaux and Remy Troulous in their sights didn't mean either man was responsible. Just because she thought this was something her ex-husband might be capable of didn't mean Frank Landers was responsible.

Who knew what acquaintances Jenny had who might want to do this? Who knew what neighbor or friend might harbor some sick twist in their mind that might have led to this?

The phone rang and Lucas snatched up the receiver, his heart pounding as it had every time the phone rang. "Hello?"

"Hi, this is Miranda Thomas with Channel Four news. I was wondering if I could speak with Mariah?"

His heart slowed once again. "She isn't taking calls."

"Who am I speaking to?" she asked.

"A 'no comment' kind of guy," he replied, and hung up the receiver.

The calls from the press had been constant, as had the calls from Richard Welch wanting updates. There had still been a few other phone messages, also—well-meaning people who wanted to know what they could do, how they could help. But so far the call Lucas most wanted hadn't come.

This time there would be no taped monologue. This time there was going to be a dialogue and maybe, just maybe, in having that dialogue Lucas could figure out what about that voice sounded so familiar.

The doorbell rang and he hurried out of the kitchen to the front door. He met Mariah coming down the hallway. She cast him a tired smile as he peeked out the door and took a step back in surprise.

"It's Remy Troulous," he said to her as he opened the door. What was he doing here?

Mariah stepped in front of Lucas. "Mr. Troulous, please come in," she said as if he were an expected, welcome friend.

Remy looked distinctly uncomfortable as he stepped through the door and into the small entry. "Please, come in and sit," Mariah said, and gestured him into the living room. "Would you like something to drink?"

"No, I'm good," he replied.

Lucas frowned at the young man. "What are you doing here, Remy?"

"I didn't want to talk to you at the office. My business is nobody's business, and I didn't want anyone to hear what I'm going to tell you." Remy's eyes gleamed with a hard edge, and he lifted his chin defensively.

"Do you know where my son is? Where Jenny is?" Mariah asked, her voice filled with urgency as she stepped closer to him.

"No." His gaze softened slightly as he looked at Mariah. "I'm sorry, but I really don't know anything about what happened to them." He looked back at Lucas. "You and I have butted heads a lot of times in the past, but even you should know this isn't my style. I don't mess with kids."

"So, what do you have to tell us?" Lucas asked.

"It's about me and Jenny."

"What about you and Jenny?" Lucas tried to hang on to his emotions.

"We were sort of seeing each other, but it's not what you think." Again Remy's chin lifted. "It wasn't anything romantic or nothing like that."

"Then what was it?" Lucas couldn't imagine what this man and his sister would have in common, why they would be seeing each other at all.

Remy shoved his hands into his pockets and gazed first at Lucas, then at Mariah, then back to Lucas. "Look, this is something I don't want anyone else to know. That's why I came here instead of telling you yesterday. You had that other dude in the room and I wasn't going to talk about it."

"Talk about what?" Lucas asked with more than a touch of impatience.

"Jenny was teaching me to read, okay? I know I can't be a gangbanger forever. I want something better, okay? But I can't do nothing about my life unless I learn how to read."

He eyed them belligerently, as if expecting them to mock or belittle his efforts. "Anyway, that's why I was meeting with her. I just thought you should know so you'll get off my back 'cause I had nothing to do with her being missing." He backed toward the door. "Sorry I can't help. I liked Jenny a lot and she was nice to me even though she didn't have to be." He dug into his pocket and pulled out a crumpled piece of paper. "This is my cell phone number. If I can do anything to help find her, give me a call."

Lucas could feel Mariah's disappointment, as rich and deep as his own. He took the piece of paper from Remy but wasn't finished with his questions. "How did you arrange this with my sister?"

Remy shrugged his narrow shoulders. "I was in the library and looking at books on reading. Jenny was in there, too, and she saw the books I was looking at. We started talking and she offered to help me. I trusted her. I knew she wouldn't tell nobody, so we met a couple of times here during the day."

"And you haven't heard anything on the streets about her disappearance?" Lucas asked.

Remy shook his head. "Nothing. Whoever took them, he ain't talking to nobody. Look, Jenny was helping me. I wouldn't have repaid her by doing something like this. I just wanted you to know." Without another word, Remy shot out of the front door.

Mariah closed the door after him and turned to face Lucas. "Do you believe him?"

"I have absolutely no reason to believe anything that falls out of that man's mouth, but yeah, I believe him."

She nodded. "So do I. It's just the kind of thing Jenny would do. I told you she would have made a great teacher."

A stab of guilt gored him. He'd been so busy worrying about the kind of woman Jenny *might* be that he hadn't taken the time to see what kind of woman she had become.

He sighed. "So, if we believe Remy, then he comes off our list of suspects."

"And since Phillip Ribideaux has done nothing suspicious in the past couple of days and we don't know where Frank is, that leaves us with nothing."

Lucas opened his mouth to protest her assessment, then closed it. Because she was right.

Chapter Ten

It had become a waiting game, and as the afternoon hours crept by, Mariah felt as if she might explode. Why didn't he call? If she and Lucas walked out the front door, would the kidnapper call then? Leave one of his cryptic messages to lead them on yet another wild-goose chase?

Lucas had remained for much of the day at the table, alternately talking on his cell phone and staring at her telephone as if willing it to ring.

Dusk was falling and the panic that night brought with it formed a big, tight lump in her chest. Another night. How many nights could she survive? How long before she lost her mind with grief?

The house had been so quiet. Until his disappearance, Mariah hadn't realized how much Billy filled up the house with sound. He often clomped when he walked, he hummed and whistled while he did his chores. And he laughed. God, what she wouldn't give to hear the sound of his laugher once again.

When the doorbell rang at seven that evening, Mariah hurried to answer it, grateful for the break from the tension, from the monotony of waiting for the kidnapper to call.

She opened the door and froze as she saw the man with a sprinkle of gray in his black hair, the narrow dark eyes that had once haunted her dreams.

"Hello, Mariah. How in the hell did you manage to lose our little boy?"

"Frank." Mariah wouldn't have thought it possible for the cold inside her to intensify, but it did at the sight of the man who had caused her such pain. A fear she thought she'd gotten past filled her.

"Your hair always looked so nice when you wore it short," he said. "Now, aren't you going to invite me in?"

Mariah felt Lucas's presence just behind her. "I don't know if she'll invite you in, but I certainly will."

As Lucas placed a hand on Mariah's shoulder, she was filled with strength. This man, this monster, couldn't hurt her ever again, and she refused to allow him to create fear inside her.

"By all means, come in," she agreed and opened the door to her past. "We've been looking for you."

"Who are you?" Frank asked Lucas as he stepped into the small foyer.

"I'm Sheriff Lucas Jamison and I have some questions for you, Frank."

"I've got questions for you. Where in the hell is my boy? What kind of an investigation is going on that a little boy and some woman have been missing for the past four days and you can't find them?"

Lucas's eyes narrowed. "Why don't we all go in and have a seat. I'll be happy to answer your questions after you've answered mine."

It was obvious Lucas intended to maintain the control in the situation. The three of them moved into the living room where Frank sat on the sofa and patted the cushion next to him with a smile at Mariah.

"When hell freezes over," she muttered under her breath and sat in the chair opposite the sofa. Lucas remained standing next to Mariah's chair.

"Can you tell me where you've been for the past four days?" Lucas asked.

Frank straightened his shoulders, as if affronted by the very question. "Surely you don't think I had anything to do with this." He glared at Mariah. "Ask her what she did to put our boy at risk. She's always been irresponsible. If anyone is at fault here, it's her."

"Right now we're talking about you," Lucas replied, his tone holding an iron edge. "I'm going to ask you again, where have you been for the past four days?"

"Up until this morning I was in my home in Shreve-port," Frank said.

"We had the authorities in Shreveport looking for you, but they couldn't find where you lived or worked," Mariah said. Funny, for so many years he'd been a monster in her mind. He'd been big and strong and scary. But now, seated on her floral-patterned sofa, he looked small and petty and nothing like a monster at all.

"I've been living with a friend and I'm between jobs at the moment. It was during breakfast this morning that I saw a newscast about Billy and Mariah and of course I came right here." He cast a sideways look at Mariah. "My new friend knows how to treat a man right."

If Mariah had to guess, his new "friend" was probably a young, impressionable woman who didn't realize the path she'd chosen when she'd hooked up with Frank Landers.

"I'll need your address in Shreveport and the name of your friend," Lucas said.

Frank's square jaw tightened. "You're wasting your time investigating me."

"It's my time to waste," Lucas replied evenly.

For the next few minutes Lucas questioned Mariah's ex-husband, and though she tried to stay focused on the conversation she found herself comparing the two men.

She'd once thought Frank the handsomest man she'd ever known, but now she saw the weakness of his jaw, the furtive cast of his eyes and the voice that radiated belligerence rather than strength.

Handsome was a man who loved his sister to distraction. Handsome was a man who had held her in his arms when she thought she might fracture. The fact that Lucas remained standing next to where she sat, creating a subtle united force to Frank, that was beyond handsome.

Somewhere in the madness of the past four days, her attitude toward Lucas Jamison had changed. As she watched the byplay between the two men, she realized she'd allowed her past to color how she saw Lucas and his actions toward Jenny.

"I demand to know exactly what's being done to find my son," Frank said, his strident tone bringing Mariah out of her thoughts. He stood as if unable to sit still another moment.

"We can discuss all that at my office," Lucas replied. "Tomorrow morning at ten. I'll meet you there and fill you in."

"Fine. I look forward to hearing what's going on." Frank headed for the front door. Mariah started to get up, but Lucas touched her shoulder.

"Stay put," he said. "I'll walk him out."

She remained in the chair and realized seeing Frank again had somehow freed her. She hadn't known until this moment that he'd still owned a part of her, that a little piece of fear still reigned in her heart where he was concerned. Facing him again had evaporated that fear, and she knew he'd never have the power in life or in dreams to scare her again.

Now if she could just get her son back…. She rose from the chair and went to the window that looked over the backyard and stared out into the deepening shadows of the night.

Strange. The wrist Frank had broken didn't ache now. Her worst nightmare had come true. Frank knew where they lived, but she wasn't running this time. He'd chased her from everything she'd known once. He wouldn't do it again. This was Billy's home. He loved it here, had friends and roots here.

She'd gone to court before to ensure that Frank had no visitation with his son. He had no legal right to be here, and this time she wasn't running.

She heard the front door open, then close. She knew when Lucas stood behind her, because she smelled the familiar scent of him. She wasn't surprised when he placed his hands gently on her shoulders and turned her around to face him.

"You okay?" he asked, his features radiating concern.

"I'm fine." She smiled. "He was my boogeyman for

so long, but seeing him now I realized he isn't anymore. He's just a pathetic little man who likes to abuse women."

"I called Agent Kessler while I was outside," Lucas said. "I want your ex-boogeyman checked inside out and upside down. I want to know everything about his movements over the past four days."

She frowned. "So you think he has Billy?"

"I think his concern for his son came off like an orchestrated act," Lucas replied. "I've definitely moved him to the top of my suspect list." He frowned. "He's a nasty piece of work." His frown fell away for a moment and a soft smile curved his lips. "But I will tell you now that you look beautiful with your long hair."

She touched his jaw, the place where a muscle knotted when he was filled with angry emotion. "I owe you an apology."

He covered her hand with his, his expression curious. "An apology for what?"

"For telling you that you remind me of Frank, for allowing you to believe that you have anything in common with that man."

A pained expression chased across his face and he dropped his hand from hers. "I would never, ever willingly hurt Jenny or any woman, but there was some truth in what you said to me." He stepped away from her and raked a hand through his hair. "I have been overbearing with Jenny. I didn't mean it to be that way, but over the past couple of days I've given it a lot of thought." His jaw knotted and his eyes darkened. "I just want a chance to do things differently."

She moved into his arms and leaned her head against

his broad chest. It scared her just a little bit, how comforting the act was, how much she felt as if she belonged in his arms.

What they were experiencing had nothing to do with real life. The connection she felt with him had been forged in circumstances of heightened emotions, of tense drama and fear. It had nothing to do with reality, and she'd be a fool to think otherwise.

Still she remained in his arms and thought of her son and his sister and wondered if there was a happy ending to be found in this mess.

Then the phone rang.

THE RING OF THE PHONE electrified Lucas. He broke their embrace and raced for the kitchen. He hit the record and speaker button, then picked up the receiver.

"Jamison," he answered.

"Ah, the good sheriff. Listen carefully. At the corner of Main and Cotton Street…"

"Wait," Lucas interrupted the kidnapper. "We need to know that Billy and Jenny are still alive. You've got to give us something."

"I reckon you've forgotten who is in charge here. At the corner of Main and Cotton Street you'll find a bench with a big wide seat."

"*Listen* to *me,* what is it you want from us?" Lucas exchanged a look of frustration with Mariah.

"At the corner of Main and Cotton…" the kidnapper began again.

"Why are you doing this? Just tell us what you want," Lucas interjected. He was trying to pull the kidnapper into a discussion, hoping that something the caller said would trigger a clue. But the kidnapper still had no desire to deviate from whatever script was in his head.

"At the corner of Main and Cotton Street, you'll find a bench with a big wide seat. If you look beneath you might find a clue, a little gift from me to you."

Lucas grunted in surprise as Mariah snatched the receiver from his hands. "Listen you, we're not playing your game anymore. You hear me? I'm done chasing around town looking for clues that aren't there." Her voice was shrill with anger and her eyes flamed with emotion. "Play your stupid game without us, because we're done."

The caller hung up.

Mariah stared at Lucas. She clutched the phone receiver so tightly her knuckles turned white. He gently tried to take it away from her.

"What have I done?" she whispered as she released the phone to him.

"You've changed the game, and that's not necessarily a bad thing," he replied.

She sank into a chair at the table and covered her face with her hands. He pulled up a chair in front of her and sat, then reached out for her hands.

"Mariah, maybe you shook him up and maybe that's what we needed to do," he said. "He's been running us all over town for nothing. It was time we told him no more. We take away the pleasure he's gotten in baiting us and maybe he'll get desperate for attention and make a mistake."

"I just hope I didn't make him angry enough to do something awful."

"If he's going to do something awful, then nothing we can do or say will make a difference," Lucas said. It was possible something awful had already been done. He couldn't ignore the possibility that Jenny and Billy had been killed in the hours immediately following the kidnapping and the killer was just amusing himself now.

"Who are you calling?" she asked as he began to punch numbers on his phone.

"The office. Ed," he said into the receiver. "I want you to do me a favor. Go to the corner of Cotton and Main and check a bench that's there. See if there's anything taped to the bottom of it, then call me back." If the kidnapper was watching, seeing the deputy might force him to act and give them something to go on.

He hung up and Mariah stared at him expectantly. "So, what do we do now?" she asked.

He shrugged and stared outside where night had once again fallen. The fourth night, and they were no closer to finding Jenny and Billy than they'd been on the first night.

He looked back at Mariah. "We do what we've been doing. We let the investigation unfold and we wait for a break."

She sighed. "Did you find out any more about Frank's whereabouts the past couple of days when you walked him outside?"

"No, but I did let him know what would happen if he bothered you while he was here in Conja Creek. I told him exactly what we thought of men who abuse women."

Her eyes widened. "You threatened him?"

"Let's just say I gave him a friendly warning."

"Did you get any feeling that he might be behind this?"

"I don't know whether he is or not, but he's the kind

of man capable of such a thing." He leaned back in the chair. "The caller's voice is so distorted it's almost impossible to match it to somebody we've heard."

"Maybe Agent Kessler will be able to tell us something about the calls," she said.

Lucas nodded. But he knew that it could take weeks, even months to get information from Kessler and his men. The FBI lab wouldn't necessarily see the kidnapping of one child and one woman from a small Southern town as a priority given all the other cases they worked.

Lucas still felt the burning need to be doing something, to tear apart the town in an effort to find the missing loved ones, but logically he knew there was nothing more to be done than what was being done.

The kidnapper was still in charge of things, and unless or until he made a mistake, there wasn't much more Lucas and his men could do.

Maylor called to let them know that there was nothing unusual about the bench at Cotton and Main. Lucas checked in with Kessler and the rest of his men, then the night stretched out before them, long and dark.

"Is your mother still alive?" he asked Mariah, seeking conversation to fill the time.

"No. She had cancer and passed away not too long after my wedding. She died happy, believing that I had found a man to love and cherish me. I'm glad she passed before she knew about Frank and about my divorce." She got up from her chair. "Want some coffee?"

"Sure," he agreed. He wished she'd sleep. What little sleep they'd both gotten over the past four days had been in unexpected catnaps, when exhaustion overwhelmed will.

As he watched her making the coffee he was struck by a burst of desire for her, a need to lose himself in her kisses, in the sweet heat her body offered.

He couldn't know if what he felt for her was real or simply emotions flaring out of control because of the situation.

It also occurred to him that, for the past four days, they'd existed like a married couple, sharing quiet conversations in the predawn moments, listening to each other breathe when the conversation ran out.

Lucas had never been a lonely man, but he had a feeling when he returned to his big house with only Marquette as company, he would be lonely. Talking to Mariah, watching her graceful movements and listening to the sound of her voice had become a pleasant habit, one he knew would be hard to break.

When the coffee was finished, she brought it to the table. She wrapped her slender fingers around her mug and eyed him curiously. "Don't you want children?"

He started to give a quick reply, but instead took a sip of coffee and thought about the question. "I haven't really thought about it for a long time. Certainly when I got married I figured eventually there would be kids. But then my marriage fell apart and I was busy raising Jenny. I didn't give it any more thought."

"Jenny is going to eventually get married and start a family of her own. That's important to her, having a husband and kids." She tilted her head a bit, the light overhead glistening in her chestnut hair. "When do you get your chance, Lucas? When is it time for you to build something just for yourself?"

"I have my work. It's always been enough for me," he replied a bit uneasily.

"Work is what I do, but being a mother is who I am." She took a sip of her coffee, then continued. "I bet you'd make an awesome dad."

He laughed, the amusement surprising even himself. "You can't have it both ways, Mariah. You've told me in so many words that I've been screwing it up with Jenny and yet you think I'd make a great dad. That's a little bit contradictory, don't you think?"

She smiled, and it was the first smile he'd seen from her that wasn't tinged with grief, that didn't hold tense lines and jagged edges. "My complaint about your parenting skills has nothing to do with when Jenny was younger. I'll bet you were a loving caretaker for her when she was a kid. My only complaint is that you don't seem to know that it's time to let go."

"Point taken," he replied. "You're different than I thought you were."

"What do you mean?"

"Whenever I saw you at the mayor's office, you seemed hard-edged and uptight. You're softer than I thought."

"I take my job very seriously. Besides, anytime you came in to see Richard, he freaked out just a little bit. I think you scare him. You're always so sure of yourself and what you're doing. Richard cares so much about this town and the people, but he's less sure about his path than you are."

"Did he know about your past? That you weren't really a widow?"

She nodded. "I had no references to give him and so

I told him the truth, that I wanted a fresh start here and was willing to work hard to create a good life. Harrington isn't my real name. I couldn't use Landers nor could I use my maiden name because I was afraid Frank would find me. Harrington is a name I chose, and the shelter where I stayed for a while helped me get identification in my new name. Richard knew all that and hired me anyway. He gave me a chance and kept my secret, and for that I'll always be grateful to him."

Lucas grinned. "Then I guess I'm going to have to ease up on Richard."

The next couple of hours passed in quiet conversation. The tension, the stress and anxiety of the past four days seemed to have momentarily ebbed, as if their minds and bodies could no longer sustain the heightened sense of fear.

She told him a little bit more about her life with Frank, her lonely childhood with her mostly absent mother, and he regaled her with tales of his life in college with the friends he called his band of brothers, the men whom he still called his friends.

It was almost midnight when the coffee was gone and the fear returned. He saw it swimming back into her eyes, in the slight shake of her hands as she removed the cups from the table.

"You should try to get some sleep," he said.

"I know. But I'm afraid to close my eyes." She placed the cups in the dishwasher then turned back to face him. "I'm afraid I'll have bad dreams, but more than that, I'm afraid those dreams might come true."

Then the phone rang again.

Chapter Eleven

Electricity sizzled through Mariah. "You think he's calling back?"

"We won't know unless we answer." He punched the record and the speaker button. "Jamison," he said.

"Lucas, it's me, Jackson." It was obvious from the background noise that Jackson Burdeaux was in his car.

"Yeah, what's up?"

"Listen, I was on my way home from a meeting and heading down Baker's Street south of town when I saw a little boy walking along the street. I've got him in my car now, but he's having trouble breathing so we're on our way to the hospital. I'm just hoping I get him there in time."

"My God. It's Billy," she said. She pushed away from the dishwasher, and a wave of dizziness struck her. She drew a deep, steadying breath. Her heart beat so fast she thought she might be having a heart attack. Billy! He was having trouble breathing, but that meant he was alive!

Lucas ended the call. "Let's go."

He didn't have to tell her twice.

"It's got to be him, right?" she asked a moment later when they were in Lucas's car. "There can't be another little boy walking along a street at midnight who has breathing problems." Hope filled her and brought tears to her eyes, yet she was afraid to believe. She was afraid the hope that now rose inside her would be smashed, and she didn't think she could survive that.

"It sounds like it's him," Lucas replied. He cast her a sideways glance. "You might want to prepare yourself. We don't know what's happened to him, where he's been. We know he's obviously suffering an asthma attack, but we don't know what else he might be suffering from."

"But surely if there's been other injuries Jackson would have mentioned them," she protested. He had to be all right. He just had to be.

"I'm not talking about physical injuries. We don't know what he's been through mentally, emotionally. He may be very fragile."

"But he's alive," she replied. Surely with enough love and time they could heal whatever might be wrong. Her mind raced with possibilities. "You mentioned that one of your college buddies is a psychiatrist."

He nodded. "Clay Jefferson. Why?"

"Does he see children? If Billy needs help, I'd want to take him to see somebody professionally." She was a jittery mess, her brain shooting in a million different directions as she mentally urged him to go faster...faster.

"One step at a time," Lucas replied as he pulled into the hospital parking lot. She was out of the car and running toward the entrance before he'd brought the car to a full halt.

Conja Creek Memorial Hospital was a small facility, mostly used for emergency situations. Most people with real health issues drove to Shreveport or were transported there.

The first person she saw as she flew through the emergency-room door was a tall, dark-haired man with slate-gray eyes. She knew in an instant this was Lucas's friend, Jackson Burdeaux. Although she wanted to thank him, her most urgent need was to see if Billy really existed behind the closed doors just ahead. She started toward the doors.

"Wait! You can't go back there." A nurse stepped in front of her, blocking her forward progress.

"Please, the little boy who was just brought in. He's my son. You have to let me through."

The nurse's implacable expression softened. "If you're his mother then we need you to sign some forms."

"Gina," Lucas's voice rang from behind them. "Let her through. The forms can wait until later."

Nurse Gina stepped aside and Mariah flew through the doors. The first person she saw sitting up on an examining table was her son.

He was being given a breathing treatment, but when he saw her he pulled the nozzle from his mouth. "Mommy," he cried as she rushed to him.

Never again would she feel the way she did at that moment, so filled with joy it nearly brought her to her knees. He was filthy and sweaty, but she wrapped her arms around him and wept with the joy of holding him.

She cried only a moment, then aware of his labored breathing she let him go and guided the nozzle of the nebulizer back to his mouth. "Breathe, honey. Just breathe."

He did as she told him, and Mariah straightened and saw Dr. Ralph Dell standing nearby. Dr. Dell was Billy's regular doctor and she hurried to where he stood.

He placed a hand on her shoulder, his wrinkled face offering her a smile. "He's going to be all right, Mariah. Other than the fact that he was scarcely breathing when Jackson brought him in, I don't see any other physical issues."

"Thank God," she replied.

"I'd like to keep him here overnight for observation. Just to be on the safe side."

"Of course. As long as I can stay with him."

Dr. Dell smiled once again. "I wouldn't have it any other way. We'll finish up his breathing treatment, then get him cleaned up and into a room."

"Did he say anything to you? About who took him?"

"He didn't offer anything and I didn't ask. My main concern was getting him treatment. He was in pretty bad shape when he was brought in. His main concern was that you were going to be mad at him."

"Mad? Why on earth would I be mad?"

"He told me he got into a stranger's car to come here and you'd always warned him never to get into a stranger's car."

Mariah's heart squeezed tight, and she left the doctor's side to return to her son. As he breathed in the medicated air that would ease his suffering, she pulled up a chair and sat next to him, then took his hand in hers.

As she held his hand she was aware of Lucas coming

to stand just behind her. He placed a hand on her shoulder and squeezed lightly. "How's he doing?"

"He's going to be fine." She smiled at her son. "They're going to keep him overnight. Did you hear that, Billy? You and I are going to stay here in the hospital for the night." He nodded.

"I'd like to have a little talk with him," Lucas said in a low voice. "I'll come back once I've spoken with Jackson," he added, as if realizing Billy would need a little time with his mother.

She didn't even notice when he drifted away, so focused was she on the sight of her son, alive and well before her.

The next half hour passed in a haze. Billy was given a second breathing treatment then washed and dressed in a gown and put in a private room.

As they arrived at the room, Mariah was surprised to see Wally seated in a chair just outside. "What are you doing here?" she asked.

"I'll be here until you and Billy get home safe and sound," he replied.

She realized Wally was a guard. Even though Billy was here, it wasn't over yet. Jenny still wasn't home, and it wouldn't be over until the guilty person was behind bars.

Finally Billy was tucked into bed, and mother and son were alone for a moment. She leaned over him and kissed his forehead, savoring the taste of his warm skin, the scent of hospital soap and precious little boy.

"I was so scared when you were gone," she said softly.

Billy gazed at his mother with big eyes. "I was scared, too, but Jenny helped. She told me not to be afraid, that her brother would find us. Has he found Jenny?"

"Not yet," Lucas said from the doorway. "I'm kind of hoping you can help me find her." He approached Billy with a smile. "I'm Lucas, Jenny's brother. Can I ask you some questions, Billy?"

"Okay," he agreed after looking at Mariah. Mariah scooted her chair closer and took his little hand in hers. She had no idea how traumatic Lucas's questioning might be, and if it became too intense she'd stop it. She'd do what was necessary to protect her son.

Lucas grabbed one of the other chairs in the room and pulled it up on the opposite side of the bed. "How are you feeling?"

"Okay now," Billy replied.

Lucas pulled a small notepad and a pen from his pocket. "Can you tell me what happened last Friday, Billy? The day you stayed home from the babysitter's because you had a sore throat?"

Billy tightened his grip on Mariah's hand, and she wanted to grab him in her arms and shield him from the trauma, from the stress of remembering. But she also knew she couldn't do that, for Jenny was still missing and their biggest lead to her now was Billy.

"Mom went to work, and me and Jenny decided to watch a movie." He looked at Mariah. "It was that new Disney movie you got me. Anyway, we'd been watching for a little while and then I had to go to the bathroom. When I came out of the bathroom Jenny was asleep on the sofa and there was a man there."

"A man? What did he look like?" Lucas leaned forward.

"I dunno. He had on a mask. You know, the kind you wear in the wintertime with just the eyes not covered. I tried to run but he caught me and he held something over my nose and mouth and I guess I fell asleep, too."

So, they now knew the kidnapping had taken place at Mariah's house, in her living room. How had he gotten in? Had the front door been unlocked? So many questions.

"And the masked man. Was he tall or short? Thin or heavy?" Lucas continued.

Billy frowned, obviously trying hard to please. "I dunno, kind of medium."

"Did you see his eyes?"

Billy hesitated, then nodded. "I'm pretty sure they were brown."

"Good, Billy. You're doing a terrific job," Lucas said. "What happened next? After you went to sleep."

"I woke up and me and Jenny were in a place." Billy's voice trembled slightly. "It was dark and I was scared, but Jenny told me not to be afraid, that you'd find us."

Lucas looked haunted by the words. "Tell me more about the place where you woke up."

"When the sun came up we could see it. It was all boarded up so we couldn't get out and there was food on a table and bottles of water. We screamed for help, but I guess nobody heard us."

"Was the man there with you?"

"No, it was just us in the little room."

"Was it a room in a house?" Lucas asked.

Billy shook his head. "Not like our house, and we could hear things at night."

"What kind of things?"

"Like big splashes and a noise that Jenny said was alligators calling to each other," Billy replied.

Mariah looked at Lucas. Once again he looked haunted, and she knew exactly what he was thinking. If Jenny was being held someplace deep in the swamp, they might never find her.

BILLY'S WORDS filled Lucas with a new kind of horror, because they confirmed his deepest fear—that Jenny was being held someplace in the swamp.

Conja Creek was nearly surrounded by swampland, with overgrown passages and areas where men hadn't been for years. It would take a hundred men days, or even weeks, to explore every inch of the swamps in search of his sister. And he knew in his gut that she didn't have days or weeks. The fact that the kidnapper had released Billy didn't bode well for Jenny.

"Billy, what happened tonight? How did you get out on the street where Mr. Burdeaux picked you up?" he asked.

"Somebody came." Billy's eyes darkened and he swallowed several times before continuing. "We heard the boat coming. I could hardly breathe, and Jenny screamed that he'd better let me go, that I was going to die if he didn't get me out of there. She told him she'd do whatever he wanted if he let me come home." Tears filled Billy's eyes. "He unlocked the door and came in. He hit Jenny. He hit her in her face, and she fell down on the floor, then he yanked me out of the room."

"And he had the mask on?" Lucas concentrated on the facts and tried to keep his emotions out of things.

But the thought of Jenny being hurt sent shards of pain slicing through him.

"Yeah, and he put me in a boat, then he covered my eyes with a blindfold. We rode for a long time in the boat then he put me into a car and we rode for a little while, then he made me get out of the car on the side of the road."

For the next hour Lucas questioned Billy, trying to get something from the boy that might lead him to his sister. It was only when Billy could no longer keep his eyes open that Lucas called a halt to the questioning.

"I'll be back tomorrow," he told Mariah as she walked him to the door. "When the doctor releases him I'll drive you both back to your place."

She nodded, her exhaustion evident in the bruiselike darkness beneath her eyes. "I'm sorry, Lucas."

He looked at her in surprise. "Sorry for what?"

"I'm sorry he didn't let them both go. I'm sorry that I have my son back and you don't have your sister. I'm sorry he couldn't tell you anything that might help you."

"But he did," Lucas replied. He drew a deep breath as he realized his emotions were precariously close to the surface. For a moment he couldn't speak as his chest filled and his throat closed with the depth of his feelings. "I thought she might already be dead. I feared they both were. What Billy told me was that she was still alive a couple of hours ago."

Mariah moved into his arms, and he grabbed onto her, surprised to find comfort in the embrace. "I'm going to find her, Mariah. I'm going to find her."

She held him for several long moments, then released him. "I know you will. Maybe after a good night's sleep Billy will remember something that will help."

He nodded and touched her cheek, her soft, smooth skin warm beneath his finger. "And now you can get some sleep, knowing that Billy is safe and where he belongs. Don't feel guilty, Mariah. Don't feel bad that Jenny hasn't come home yet. Rejoice in your son's safe return. Please, you have to do that for me."

Without another word he walked out of the hospital room. Wally sat in a chair just outside the door, a magazine in his lap. "Don't let anyone in but the doctor or a nurse," Lucas said. "And I want a list of anyone who tries to get in to see either Billy or Mariah."

Wally nodded. "Did he give you anything?"

"Not enough," Lucas replied, a ball of emotion knotted tight in his chest. "If you need me, I'll be at the office. Agent Kessler and I are going to coordinate." He started to walk away, but paused and returned to Billy's hospital room doorway and looked in.

Mariah was in the bed with her son, her arms around him as they both slept. Thank God. Thank God Billy was okay and back where he belonged. It certainly hadn't been through any efforts on Lucas's part.

What had prompted the kidnapper to let Billy go? If it had been Billy's health issue, then it was obvious the kidnapper didn't want to be responsible for his death. Or maybe it had been Mariah's challenge to the kidnapper, her refusal to play his game any longer.

As Lucas headed out of the hospital, he realized he couldn't remember when he'd last slept. His eyes felt gritty, but there was no way he was going to sleep now. He needed to catch up with Kessler and coordinate some sort of search.

"At least we know we can strike Frank Landers off

our list of suspects," Kessler said two hours later. "Ben has been sitting on him and said he hasn't left his hotel all day. He couldn't have been the man who got Billy and then dropped him off on the side of the road."

"I'd already pretty much written him off anyway," Lucas replied. "He likes to hurt defenseless women, but he doesn't have the nerve to pull off something like this." Lucas cast a weary hand across his eyes.

"Go home, Lucas," Kessler said. "There's nothing more we can do tonight. You need some sleep. Tomorrow we'll get everyone we can out searching."

Although Lucas wanted to protest, he knew Kessler was right. Nothing more could be done without the light of day. The adrenaline that had filled him when he'd known Billy had been found was gone, leaving behind a weariness the likes of which he'd never known.

As he drove home, Billy's words tormented him. *He hit her in the face.* What did that mean? Had he blackened her eye, broken her jaw? Was she now bleeding and in pain? The very idea of somebody laying hands on Jenny created a rage of mammoth proportions inside him.

Who was behind this? Somehow he didn't think the kidnapper was just going to let Jenny go as he had done Billy. The kidnapper wanted something, and the most frightening thing of all was that Lucas had a feeling Jenny's very life depended on him figuring it out.

His house was empty and silent when he arrived. Marquette had gone home hours ago and wouldn't be back until morning. He checked his watch. It was after three; morning would be here soon.

He fell into bed without showering or taking off his clothes. He stretched out on top of the bedspread and was asleep in minutes.

The dream came almost immediately. Jenny, her face black-and-blue, crying out to him. "Lucas, help me. You have to find me before it's too late."

Lucas walked along the edge of dark, murky swamp water. Nearby an alligator bellowed, and gnarled cypress trees rose up like twisted, sun-bleached skeletons. "Where are you, Jenny?" he yelled. He had to find her, before it was too late. He had to save her; he needed to save her.

"I'm sorry, Lucas. I'm sorry I've been such a pain in your life." Her voice was faint, as if she'd given up hope. "I love you, Lucas."

"I love you," he yelled back. "Jenny, I'm the one who is sorry. Do you hear me? I'm sorry." He waited for a reply, for the sound of her voice drifting to him. But there was nothing, no answering cry.

"Jenny!" he screamed. "Jenny, where are you?" The only reply was a second roar from the alligator.

He sat up, his heart banging with ferocity against his ribs. He looked toward the window where dawn had already broken through night clouds. The clock on his nightstand read almost six. He'd slept for three hours, albeit a sleep filled with nightmares.

He exited the shower and sensed Marquette had arrived. The scent of frying bacon and freshly brewed coffee filled the air as he descended the grand staircase and headed for the kitchen.

"Sit. You aren't getting out of this house without a good breakfast," Marquette commanded. "I might be old but I'll wrestle you to the ground before I'll let you leave here without eating." She pointed to the small oak table where a place setting had already been laid. "Lord knows when was the last time you had a decent meal." She poured him coffee, then returned to the stove.

"Billy was found last night wandering along a highway," he said as he sat.

"I heard." Marquette forked the cooked bacon out of the skillet as Lucas looked at her in surprise.

"It didn't happen until late. How did you hear about it?" he asked.

"Got a call this morning from Levina. Her daughter has a friend who knows a nurse over at Memorial." Marquette broke three eggs into the skillet.

"Ah, nice to know the gossip grapevine in Conja Creek is alive and well," he replied dryly.

"That it is," she agreed easily. "I also heard that Billy wasn't much help in letting you know where our little girl is."

"All he could tell me was that they were being held someplace in the swamp."

Marquette's eyes were as dark as he'd ever seen them as she placed his plate in front of him. "If that's the truth, then how will you ever find her?"

"I'll search until I do," he replied, a knot of tension twisting in his stomach. Marquette knew how futile a search might be, how long it would take to explore each and every inch of the swampland, but thankfully she didn't say anything to remind him of that.

"Why would he release Billy and not let Jenny go?" she asked.

Lucas frowned. "That's the million-dollar question

at the moment." He took a sip of his coffee and eyed the morning newspaper that was next to his plate, still rolled with a rubber band.

He took another sip of coffee then removed the band from the paper, opened it and gasped. The headline read, Two Victims at Risk While Sheriff Plays in the Park.

There was a full-size color picture of Lucas and Mariah in the park. The photo told a false tale, implying some sort of romantic liaison.

Mariah was in his arms and it looked as if they were sharing an intimate embrace. In truth, he'd been consoling Mariah after she'd dug up most of the flower bed looking for a clue. And the kidnapper had not only been there, but he'd taken a photo, a photo specifically chosen to imply ineptitude.

It spoke of Lucas's inadequacies as a law enforcement official, reminding the readers that he'd arrested the wrong man in the Bennett murder case and now couldn't even find a little boy and his own sister.

Lucas really wasn't surprised. The Conja Creek newspaper was something of a joke, offering up tabloid-type stories along with the daily news. Owner Sam Rinkin wouldn't have a problem running a story that made Lucas look bad, despite an anonymous source. Lucas had run for sheriff against Sam's brother in the last election and when Lucas won, the Rinkin brothers hadn't hidden their animosity.

It was public humiliation spread across the front page of the *Conja Creek Gazette*. But more than that, it answered a question that had burned in Lucas's heart since the moment he'd realized Billy and Jenny were in trouble.

He'd wondered if the kidnapping had been about Mariah, or if it had been about Jenny. But now he knew the truth. It wasn't about either of them.

It was about him.

Chapter Twelve

Mariah stared at the morning paper in horror. Billy still slept in the hospital bed. She'd awakened surprisingly early considering the time they'd finally gone to sleep.

She'd remained in bed for a long time after opening her eyes, listening to Billy's easy breathing and thanking the stars that he was where he belonged—in her arms. She'd crept out of the bed without awakening him.

As much as she rejoiced that Billy was home safe and sound, her heart was still heavy, since Jenny remained in danger and Lucas was without any real answers.

She sat in the chair next to Billy's bed and sipped the coffee a nurse had been kind enough to bring to her a few minutes earlier. The article that accompanied the photo was scathing, an indictment against Lucas for incompetence. It rehashed the murder of Erica Bennett and reminded the readers that Lucas had arrested the wrong man for the murder. Mariah knew the truth about the arrest of Sawyer for his wife's crime, that Mayor Welch had pressured Lucas to make the arrest.

Of course it was all ridiculous, and she couldn't believe that Samuel Rinkin, the owner of the paper, had run both the photo and the article without even asking for a comment from either her or Lucas.

She tossed the paper on the floor next to her chair and instead watched Billy sleep. The rhythmic rise and fall of his chest was reassuring, as was the absence of any ominous wheeze.

Although he hadn't spoken much about the days he'd been held captive, he didn't appear to be unduly emotionally stressed now that he was home. His main concern appeared to be for his friend, Jenny.

Mariah prayed there were no emotional scars left from this ordeal, and she prayed that Jenny would come home soon. She turned her attention to the window, where the sun was just beginning to peek over the horizon.

Had Lucas seen the paper yet? What was going through his mind? Through his thoughts? It was so unfair for him to be damned by a photo that was twisted and perverted into something other than what it was.

She picked up the paper once again and stared at the photograph, remembering those moments when Lucas had held her together as she broke apart.

Lucas was nothing like the man she'd once thought he was. In Frank's case she'd mistaken dominance for strength, control for love. But in Lucas's case she'd done the exact opposite. She'd damned him with the taint of her past. There was no question she still believed he needed to give Jenny more space, an opportunity to make her own decisions, but there was not an abusive bone in Lucas's body.

She frowned as she spied a small insert at the bottom of the front page, indicating an interview with one of the victims' father on page three. She flipped the pages and found the article. Frank had given an interview as the loving, caring father.

He'd depicted himself as having a close relationship with his son despite his divorce from Mariah. Lies, all lies. It had been obvious that, at the time they had interviewed him, Frank had believed that Billy was already dead. She wadded up the page and threw it in the corner with disgust.

An hour later she was still seated at the window, while Billy remained sleeping, when she heard a commotion in the hallway.

"I said you can't go in there," Wally's voice drifted from the closed door.

"That's my son in there and nobody is going to stop me from seeing him." Frank's voice radiated the kind of simmering rage Mariah knew well. But this time she felt no fear. After all she'd been through in the past week, she knew Frank Landers could never frighten her again.

Checking to make certain that Billy was still asleep, she walked to the door, opened it and stepped out, then pulled it closed behind her.

Frank glared at her. "I want to see my son."

"The sheriff says nobody goes in, so nobody goes in, and that includes you," Wally exclaimed, his meaty fists clenched at his sides.

"Do something," Frank demanded of Mariah. "Tell him I have a right to see my son."

"You have no rights here, Frank, and you particularly

don't have the right to see the son you never wanted."
Memories assailed her, memories of how angry Frank
had been when she'd become pregnant, how during her
pregnancy he'd acted as though the child had nothing
to do with him. "You don't scare me anymore, Frank
and there's nothing for you here. Go back to wherever
you came from and just leave us alone."

"That's not fair. I didn't know where you were, how
to find you. I figured you changed your name and
probably got some illegal identification. How was I
supposed to go about finding you?"

"I did change my name, but you had my social
security number." She stared at the man who had
haunted her dreams, the man she'd been afraid would
hunt her down. "You *figured* I'd changed my name? You
never even looked for us." The truth slammed into her
and was there in the sheepish expression on his face.

She laughed, unable to stop herself. God, she'd been
afraid for so long and she suddenly realized she hadn't
hidden herself at all. She'd been a fool without a real
plan when she'd left him.

She'd been living a mere five hours from Frank,
using her own social security number. If he'd hired a
good private investigator, even if he'd just looked
himself, she would have been found in a matter of
hours. But Frank hadn't cared to look. All this time
she'd been afraid of a ghost.

And she'd hidden not only from Frank, but from the
people of Conja Creek, who had embraced her. There
would be no more lies. No more hiding away. She was
confident that the friends she'd made here would still
be her friends when they learned the truth about her past.

"Go home, Frank," she said. "I'll spend every dime I have, fight you tooth and nail before I'll let you see Billy. We're out of your life, now get out of ours."

"You heard the lady," Wally said. "Get on out of here before I arrest you for being stupid."

Frank glared at them both, then turned on his heels and disappeared down the hallway. Mariah wasn't sure but she had the distinct feeling she'd seen the last of him. Without her fear to feed him, he'd have no further interest in her or Billy. And Billy had expressed time and again that he didn't want to spend time with his father, although when he came of age, it would be up to him.

"Thank you, Wally," she said to the deputy.

"My pleasure, ma'am," he said with a wink.

She turned and went back into the room where Billy still slept. It was after ten when he finally opened his eyes. "Did they find Jenny yet?" he asked.

"Not yet, but I'm sure everyone is looking really hard to find her." Mariah pulled her chair up next to his bed. She was certain if anything had happened overnight Lucas would have let her know.

She wondered when he'd show up here. He'd said he'd be here to take her and Billy home and she was eager to talk to him about the newspaper article.

As Billy ate breakfast she was grateful to see that his appetite was good, and although he talked a little bit about his time in captivity, he seemed more focused on all the things he wanted to do when he got back home. She thought it was a good sign. He was looking toward the future and not to the past.

What little he did say about his time away let Mariah

know that Jenny had worked overtime to try to keep him from being afraid. She'd put her very life on the line to try to bargain Billy's release. They *had* to find her, Mariah thought with a sense of desperation.

It was just after noon when Lucas walked in. The first thing Mariah noticed was that although he was dressed in a neatly pressed uniform, he looked more exhausted than she'd ever seen him. Still, he offered her and Billy a bright smile. "Hey, buddy, how you doing this morning?" he asked Billy.

"Good, but I want to go home. I've missed seeing my friends and stuff."

"The doctor was just in and released him. They're doing the discharge paperwork now," Mariah explained.

Lucas nodded and pulled something from his pocket. "Billy, I brought you something," he said. He held out a small gold badge. "Since you were so much help answering my questions yesterday I've decided to make you my official deputy."

"Wow!" Billy's eyes lit up as he took the badge from Lucas. "Thank you, this is way cool."

Mariah's heart expanded. With everything that Lucas had going on, he'd thought about a badge for Billy, instinctively knowing that an eight-year-old boy would love the idea of being an official deputy.

"Why don't you give it to me and when you're dressed we'll pin it on your shirt," Mariah suggested.

"And I can wear it whenever I want, right?" Billy asked.

Mariah smiled as she placed the badge on the table next to the bed. "You'll have to take it off when you take a bath, but other than that you can wear it all the time."

"Are you up to answering a few more questions, Deputy Billy?" Lucas asked.

"Sure," Billy said as he sat up straighter in the bed.

For the next half hour Lucas asked Billy the same questions he'd asked him the night before. Mariah knew that Lucas was hoping something new would come to light, but Billy couldn't tell him any more than he had the previous night.

Mariah watched the exchange between her son and the sheriff, not surprised by the gentleness Lucas displayed when asking difficult questions. He was good with Billy and Billy responded to him with an eagerness to please.

She could smell Lucas's familiar scent, the cologne and soap scent one she would forever identify with him. What agony he must be going through. The fact that Billy had been released and Jenny had not been seemed so evil, so ominous.

"Why don't you go ahead and get dressed," Mariah suggested after the nurse dropped off the discharge papers. "Sheriff Jamison and I will be just outside the door."

She and Lucas stepped outside the door to let Billy have his privacy. "Where's Wally?" Mariah asked, noting that both Wally and the chair he had sat in were gone.

"I sent him home. He told me you had a little confrontation with Frank. He said you were awesome."

Mariah smiled. "I don't know how awesome I was, but he won't be haunting my dreams anymore."

"Ben called me a little while ago and said Landers checked out of the motel and headed out of town."

"I pity whatever woman he's living with now." She

took one of his hands and pressed it between hers. "How are you doing? You look exhausted."

"I'm tired," he admitted. "Agent Kessler is coordinating a search of the swamp and I'm just hoping they'll find her." For a moment his eyes were dark and tortured. "So, how does it feel to be front-page news?" he asked.

She grimaced and dropped his hand. "That wasn't news, that was tabloid nonsense. I can't believe Sam Rinkin allowed it into his paper."

"I had a chat with Sam a little while ago," Lucas replied. "He told me the photo and the article showed up in a plain brown envelope yesterday afternoon. He didn't see who left it, thinks it might have been left while he was at lunch. And I'll be checking Sam's and his brother's alibis for the day of the kidnapping."

He frowned, the gesture emphasizing the tired lines on his face. "But at least I now know something about this case. I know it was never about you or Jenny, that it's about me. Somebody wants to discredit me as sheriff, somebody hates me enough that they kidnapped my sister." His dark eyes were bleak as he gazed at Mariah. "I just have to hope that they don't hate me enough to kill Jenny," he said softly.

LUCAS HAD HOPED that in questioning Billy again the little boy might remember something that would point to a specific location in the swamp, but he'd gotten no more from Billy today than he had the night before.

As he drove Mariah and Billy home, he realized the weight of his grief was far different now than it had been the day before. While Billy had been missing he'd managed to keep his focus on the little boy. But now that Billy was home safe and sound, Jenny filled Lucas's thoughts, his heart, and there was nothing to mitigate his pain.

As he drove he listened to Billy talking about Jenny and the time they'd shared in the shanty. It was obvious that Jenny had acted the part of hero, setting aside her own fears to soothe Billy's.

Pride filled Lucas's heart. He would have guessed that Jenny would fall apart, that she would be hysterical, but she'd managed to hold it together for the sake of a little boy. Mariah was right, Jenny was much stronger than he'd ever given her credit.

When they reached Mariah's place Ben was waiting for them on the front porch. "What's he doing here?" Mariah asked.

"I think it would be a good idea if I keep a deputy here for the next couple of days," he replied.

"You really think that's necessary?" she asked softly.

He parked the car in the driveway and turned off the engine. "I'm not sure. I know you want to think this is all over for you, but I'd rather be safe than sorry."

"This won't be over for me until Jenny is home safely. This won't be over until the guilty person is rotting in jail," she replied.

They got out of the car and Ben rose from his chair on the porch. "Hi, Sheriff, Mariah." He squatted down to Billy's height. "I understand you're the new deputy in town."

Billy grinned and nodded his head, touching the badge he wore proudly on his shirt. Mariah turned and looked at Lucas. "Are you coming in?"

He hesitated a moment, then nodded. "Maybe for

just a few minutes." He wanted to talk to her about the thoughts whirling in his head.

The minute they entered the house Billy ran to his bedroom, then came back into the kitchen and asked if he could watch a movie. With him happily entertained by his favorite Disney film, Lucas and Mariah sat at the kitchen table.

"I've told you all along that something about those recorded messages sounded familiar to me but I couldn't put my finger on what it was," he said as she poured them each a cup of freshly brewed coffee.

"And you have now?"

He shook his head in frustration. "No, I still can't figure it out, but I know from the newspaper article that the kidnapper is somebody close to me, somebody I know on a personal level, and it's hatred of me that's driving this train."

"So you think Billy was never the intended victim?" she asked.

"On most days when you're at work, Billy is at the babysitter's. I think the kidnapper intended to take Jenny all alone and Billy just happened to be at the wrong place at the wrong time."

"Do you have any idea who might hate you that badly?" she asked. "Maybe somebody you've arrested in the past?"

He shrugged. "Agent Kessler and I spent the morning going over my files, looking for a likely suspect, but nobody popped out." He leaned back in the chair and studied her for a long moment, then leaned forward once again. "You don't think this is something our good mayor might be behind?"

Her eyes radiated her shock at his words. They widened and blinked in surprise. "Richard? Why on earth would Richard want to do something like this?"

He shrugged again. "It's no secret that he and I don't see eye to eye. We butt heads on a regular basis and I'm sure he feels his life would be much easier if he didn't have to contend with me."

"Richard has trouble remembering to pick his shirts up at the cleaners, I can't imagine him being capable of pulling together something like this. According to Billy, that shanty was stocked with food and water. Somebody spent a lot of time planning this. Richard can't plan his own lunch hour, let alone a crime."

This was why Lucas had wanted to talk to her, because of her intelligence, because he trusted her judgment, and at the moment he didn't know who else he could trust.

"It was just a thought." He drank his coffee, then stood. "I've got to get back to the office."

"You need to go to bed," she replied. "You're exhausted and you can't help Jenny if you crash and burn."

"I know, I'll get a couple hours of sleep later." He was afraid to sit too long in the comfort of her kitchen, was afraid that if he stayed inert for too long, he *would* crash and burn.

Somebody close to him.

Somebody close. The words echoed in his head as he drove back to the office. The newspaper article was obviously meant to humiliate him, to make him appear ineffective to the taxpayers he served. Did the kidnapper want him to resign? To lose his position? Who had anything to gain by that?

Although Mariah had been quick to proclaim Richard's innocence, he still considered the mayor as viable a candidate as anyone. Richard might come off as a buffoon, but he'd been smart enough to get himself elected.

The only other person at the office was Louis, who was manning the desk. "Hey, Sheriff," he said. "I figured you were out on one of the search boats."

"I wanted to interview Billy again, so I went to the hospital and picked up him and Mariah to take them home." Lucas moved to his desk and sat.

"Did you get anything more from him?" Louis asked.

"No, nothing more than I got last night." He leaned back in the chair and fought the overwhelming sense that it was too late. For all he knew the kidnapper had already killed Jenny and fed her to the gators that Billy had heard bellowing outside the place they'd been held.

Don't give up, a small voice whispered inside. But with each moment that passed, it was getting more and more difficult to hang on to hope.

"No more calls?" Louis asked, pulling Lucas from his dark thoughts.

"No. I'm making a calculated guess that he won't call at Mariah's place anymore. With Billy home I think she's been taken out of the game. If he calls, he'll call me on my cell phone like he did the very first time he contacted us."

"So, what are you doing here?" Louis asked.

"I was going to go through some more files, see if I can find somebody who pops out at me, somebody who might want to see me punished in some way."

One of Louis's black eyebrows rose. "Is that what you think this is about? Punishment?"

"I didn't before the newspaper article this morning. I assume you saw it."

Louis nodded. "A bunch of crap, if ever I saw crap. You're a good sheriff, Lucas. I can't think of another man I'd rather work for."

Louis's loyalty soothed Lucas somewhat and raised a lump of emotion in his throat. "Thanks, I appreciate it. I've tried to be good for this town."

For the next four hours Lucas pored over his files, compiling a list of names. He asked Deputy Ed Maylor to bring him a burger for dinner, then continued going over lists, taking off names and adding others.

At dusk he headed to the small town dock to wait for the search boats. As he stood at the end of the wooden structure, his heart was heavier than it had ever been. He'd been so focused on Mariah's pain it had been easy to stuff his own away. But now he felt as if he were bleeding from the inside out, bleeding for a sister he recognized he might never see again.

The sun dipped lower, casting the surrounding swamp in deep shadows. Mosquitoes began to swarm, the incessant buzzing enough to drive a sane person mad. He felt half-mad as he waited. Mad with grief for a sister he feared was dead.

The boats began to arrive, the search parties hot and weary from battling the swamp. Most of the men refused to meet Lucas's eyes as they disembarked, and he knew they held little hope of a happy ending.

Sawyer Bennett was on the second boat, and he walked to where Lucas stood. "How you holding up?"

"As well as can be expected," Lucas replied.

"That newspaper article this morning, I just wanted you to know that folks around here trust you, Lucas. They know you're a good man and you're the person they want as their sheriff."

Lucas looked at the man he considered one of his best friends. "I arrested you for Erica's murder, and you weren't guilty."

Sawyer nodded. "You did what you had to do. Despite our friendship, you followed the damning evidence and did what was right. Besides, in the end it all worked out okay. I don't harbor a grudge, Lucas. I respect what you did."

Once again a knot of emotion crawled up into Lucas's throat. "Thanks, Sawyer. I appreciate your support."

Sawyer held out a hand and when Lucas grabbed it, Sawyer pulled him into a bear hug. "You'll get through this," he said, then released Lucas.

It was dark when the last boat pulled in. Nothing more could be done until morning. As Lucas got into his car and headed toward his house, he was suffused with a chill despite the hot mugginess of the night air that blew into his car window.

Flashes of Jenny filled his mind. He saw her as a young girl, putting on a play just for him, heard the ring of her laughter in his head. He'd built his life around taking care of her, and he couldn't imagine life without her.

It wasn't until he parked his car that he realized he hadn't driven home. Instead he had driven to Mariah's house. A light spilled out of the front window, and Ben sat in his car at the curb.

Lucas got out of his car, his weariness making it difficult for him to put one foot in front of the other. He walked to Ben's car and greeted his deputy. "Go home," he said. "I'll get somebody here to take over, but you go home and get some sleep."

Ben didn't wait to be told twice. He started his engine and pulled away from the curb. Lucas watched him go, then turned and stared at Mariah's front door.

Why was he here? Why hadn't he gone home? He pushed himself forward and lightly tapped on her door. She opened it. Her soft curly hair spilled around her shoulders, and her blue eyes radiated gentle concern as she looked at him. She wore the terry-cloth robe she'd had on the night they'd made love. That night seemed as if it was a million years ago.

It was at that moment that Lucas realized he was falling in love with her, and he knew there would be no happy ending here, either. When this was all over, he feared that to her he would be just a bad memory of the worst time in her life.

Chapter Thirteen

He looked like death.

Lucas's eyes held an emptiness that might have been frightening had she not known what put it there, had she not experienced it herself.

"Lucas," she said softly.

He gazed at her in bewilderment. "I was on my way home. I don't know what I'm doing here."

She took him by the hand and pulled him inside the door. She knew where he was. He was in that same place she had been when she'd been digging up the flower bed in the park. He was in a place beyond grief, outside of despair, a place made worse by his obvious physical exhaustion.

She pulled him through the living room and started down the hallway, but he stopped and gazed at her with his dead, dark eyes. "Wha...what are you doing?"

"I'm putting you to bed," she said briskly.

"What about Billy?" he asked.

"He's sleeping and that's exactly what you need." She tugged his hand and he followed. When they reached her bedroom she dropped his hand. "Get undressed," she said briskly.

He hesitated only a moment, then did as she asked. As he took off his clothing, stripping to his briefs, she pulled down the spread.

She tried to keep herself focused on the task at hand and not on his near nakedness. She tried not to notice his long muscled legs and the width of his tanned chest. At the moment, he didn't need her. What he needed more than anything was the healing power of sleep.

He was like a docile child as she motioned him into the bed. He got beneath the covers and closed his eyes, a deep sigh escaping from him. He was asleep before she left the room.

Mariah went into Billy's room and stood at the side of his bed. Her son slept deeply. She often joked with him that a bomb could go off beneath his bed and he wouldn't wake up.

She listened to the reassuring sound of his regular breathing. She'd stopped believing in miracles a long time ago, but it was nothing short of miraculous that Billy was home and sleeping peacefully in his own bed.

She left his room, checked to make sure the doors were all locked, then went to her bedroom and shrugged out of her robe. Lucas was sound asleep, a faint snore coming from him.

Funny that she'd misjudged Frank. She'd just assumed that he would hunt her down like a dog, unable to let her go. Instead he'd simply found another victim.

She'd misjudged Lucas, as well. He was a good man, with a good heart, a heart that at the moment was beating in limbo, someplace between hope and heartbreak.

She gazed at Lucas. A small frown furrowed the skin between his eyes as if even sleep couldn't banish the all-consuming worry his heart carried. His long, dark lashes rested against dark shadows beneath his eyes. When would this end? And at the end of it all, would he be a broken man?

She crawled into the bed next to him and found the sound of his snoring oddly comforting. He lay on his side and she spooned him, hoping the warmth of her body against his would somehow comfort him.

Within minutes she was asleep. She awakened much later, surrounded by warmth and the achingly familiar scent of Lucas. At some point in the night they had shifted positions. He now spooned her and his hand caressed up and down her hip in a slow, delicious stroke as his mouth pressed hotly against her neck.

She leaned against him, letting him know she was awake, and his hand moved up to cup her breast. Her breath caught as his thumb brushed over her nipple, causing rivulets of heat to spiral through her. He kissed and nipped the back of her neck, down to the middle of her shoulders, sparking a need in her.

She turned to face him and, in the predawn light that spilled through the window, she saw the naked hunger, his need for her in his eyes.

There was no way she could deny him, nor did she want to. She wanted him as badly as he wanted her. She placed a hand on his jaw. His whiskers were slightly rough beneath her touch and she ran her hand from there down into the silky hair that darkened his chest.

His mouth moved to capture the tip of one of her breasts, and she tangled her hands in his hair, urging him closer...closer still.

They made love gently, quietly, coming together easily

and fitting as if they belonged. Lucas's mouth tasted every inch of her skin, taking her again and again to the edge of madness but not allowing her complete release.

She did the same with him, using her hands and her mouth to explore his body, enjoying the soft sounds of his moans and sighs.

She had no illusions about the lovemaking, knew that Lucas was reaching for life, rather than reaching for her. She suspected she could have been any woman in the bed next to him and his need would be just as great. But that didn't matter to her. She just wanted to be here for him.

It didn't take long for their movements to become more frantic. She reached her peak first, spinning out of control with the pleasure that washed over her in wave after wave. Almost immediately he stiffened against her and cried out her name as he found his own release.

They remained entwined, hearts slowing with passion spent. He finally looked at her, his eyes dark and unreadable. "That was a major mistake," he said.

The words pierced through her with unexpected pain. He must have seen something in her expression, for he quickly added, "I didn't use any protection."

"Don't worry, I'm on the pill." She'd been on the pill since Billy had been born and hadn't stopped taking it with her divorce.

He studied her features for a long moment and looked as if he wanted to say something. "What?" she asked.

He shook his head. "Nothing." He placed his fingers against her cheek in the familiar gesture she'd come to cherish. "Thank you, not necessarily for the lovemaking, but for being a safe place for me to fall." He glanced to the clock on her nightstand. "I've got to get going. Mind if I use your shower?"

"Help yourself." As he left the room she rolled onto her back and stared at the ceiling.

Despite the beauty of what they had just shared, she had a bad feeling about things. If Lucas was right and all of this had really been about hatred for him, then what incentive did the kidnapper have to let Jenny live?

IT WAS JUST AFTER NINE when Lucas returned to his office. Mariah had insisted he not leave her house without breakfast, so she'd made him and Billy pancakes.

The breakfast had been a glimpse into a home life Lucas had always lacked. A moment of time—first thing in the morning—shared with people you cared about, people who cared about you.

Billy was a charmer, and Lucas could easily understand how Jenny had fallen in love with the kid. His little gold badge had been pinned to his pajamas when he'd come to the table, and during the meal he'd talked about wanting to be a sheriff when he grew up.

But the moment Lucas walked into his office, breakfast became only a vague, pleasant memory as he greeted Wally, who manned the front desk, and Agent Kessler, seated at one of the other desks.

Search teams had gone out once again at daybreak, and for the next hour Kessler and Lucas compared notes, read reports and interviews and tried to come up with something, anything concrete.

At noon Lucas was alone in the office. Kessler and

Wally had walked to the café for lunch, but Lucas wasn't interested in food.

He leaned back in his chair and closed his eyes, working what few facts they knew through his mind. Nothing made sense. He couldn't get a handle on things. He opened his eyes and began to make a list of new people to interview and check out alibis.

Richard Welch went to the top of the list, followed by two local thugs that Lucas had arrested a month before for attempted car theft.

He knew he was grasping at straws, but didn't have anything else to hang on to. Every place they turned seemed to lead to a dead end, but Lucas knew that somebody close to him, perhaps somebody he liked and trusted, was behind the kidnapping.

When his cell phone rang, he practically jumped out of his chair, but the caller ID showed that it was Ed Maylor. "What's up?" he asked.

"Figured I'd check in. I'm sitting on Ribideaux, but I think he's a dead end. He's moved into his new apartment and doesn't seem to be doing anything suspicious."

"I've got another assignment for you," Lucas said. "I want you to check up on Tebo Wales and Junior Tanner, see what they've been doing for the past week." Maylor could follow up on the two thugs. Lucas wanted to question Richard Welch himself.

"I reckon I can take care of a couple of lowlifes," Ed replied.

"Good, check in with me when you're finished."

Lucas hung up and frowned thoughtfully. Something niggled in the back of his brain. He stared at the phone. What was it? Something…something just on the edge of his consciousness.

He needed to hear the tapes again. Something was there…something important. He felt it in his gut.

He moved over to the desk Kessler had been using. Recording equipment was set up for listening to the taped messages the kidnapper had left.

"Touching scene in the cemetery," the kidnapper's voice rang out. Lucas hit the Stop button and fast forwarded.

"…by the twisted tree."

Again he hit Forward, wondering what it was that had a burst of adrenaline soaring through him, a frantic thrum to his heartbeat.

"I reckon you've forgotten who is in charge here. At the corner of Main and Cotton Street you'll find a bench with a big wide seat."

Lucas stopped it and played it again. "I reckon you've forgotten who is in charge here."

He played two words over and over again.

"I reckon…"

"I reckon…"

He stopped the machine, his heart pounding so loudly he could hear it in his head. *I reckon I can take care of a couple of lowlifes. I reckon the kidnapper figures Lucas can pay big bucks to get his sister back safe and sound.*

He released a low gasp as he thought of his deputy. Ed? Ed Maylor? Although he didn't want to believe it, he couldn't deny that the voice on the tape, in speaking those two single words, had a rhythm just like Ed's.

Ed lived a quiet life alone in an apartment in town,

and there was no other reason for Lucas to think he was guilty except that damning tape and a strong gut feeling that had now moved to a shout in his brain.

Jumping up from his desk, he left the office and walked the short distance to the café. The place was jumping with noontime diners, but he easily spied Wally and Kessler in a booth near the back. He slid into the booth next to Kessler and looked at Wally, who had given Ed a personal recommendation at the time he'd been brought on as a deputy.

"Tell me what you know about Ed Maylor," he said without preamble.

Kessler sat up straighter in his seat as Wally stared at Lucas in confusion. "What do you want to know?" he asked curiously.

"Has he ever mentioned having a beef with me?" Lucas asked.

"No, why? Is there a problem?"

"I don't know. And whatever we say stays here. I don't want any of the other men to know what we're talking about here," Lucas said. If he was wrong, he didn't want to taint Ed's reputation, ruin his career with misplaced suspicions.

"What else do you know about him?"

"He's swamp people, like me," Wally said. "From what I know his mama and daddy weren't much good. They lived someplace deep in Black Bay until Ed was a teenager and left the swamp. From what he told me, one day he went to visit them and they were gone. Ed was determined to make something of himself. He's worked hard to put the smell of the swamp behind him."

"Black Bay. You know where in Black Bay?" Lucas

asked. That particular area of the swamp was difficult to travel, with almost impassable channels.

"No, I'm not sure. What's going on, Lucas?"

"We need to get a boat." Lucas pulled his cell phone from his pocket. "And I'm calling Remy Troulous to see if he'll guide us in. That boy knows the swamp better than anyone."

"What about Maylor? You think he's behind this? You want me to pick him up?" Kessler asked.

"No, I want you both with me in the boat in case there's a situation if and when we find this place. We'll worry about Maylor later. I could be wrong about him, but if I'm right, then I want to be the one to bring him in."

"BLACK BAY IS the devil's playground," Remy said an hour later as the four of them took off in a boat Remy had borrowed from a friend. "Gators are bigger and meaner there, and you can feel the evil in the air."

He manned the motor, steering them easily through the murky, dark water. "There's so many channels rumor has it that fishermen don't even come in here for fear of getting lost."

He grinned at Lucas, that charming arrogant grin that was his trademark. "Who would have thought I'd live long enough to have the sheriff call me for help."

"Just get us through Black Bay," Lucas said. He turned to Wally. "Ed ever tell you exactly where in here his parents lived?"

Wally shook his head. "He just told me it was a stinking shanty that he couldn't wait to forget."

It didn't take long before they were traveling those

half-choked channels. The heat was stifling and the humidity made it difficult to draw a full breath.

Lucas's thoughts were as dark as the murky water that surrounded them. *You're too late,* a little voice whispered in the back of his head. When he released Billy, Maylor had probably killed Jenny.

That's why the caller hadn't phoned again. Because the game was over and Lucas was the loser. His heart hurt, and he closed his eyes against the pain and summoned up a picture of Mariah in his head. It was easier to think of Mariah than it was to picture his sister dead.

In his mind's eye he saw Mariah's features, soft with a smile, as they had been at breakfast that morning. He heard the ring of her laughter, remembered how she'd given to him in bed as if feeding a primitive need of his.

He'd like to think that when this was all over, they could continue to see each other, build on the crazy relationship that had sprung up between them, but in his heart he had little hope for that. Aside from her telling him that he reminded her of her abusive ex-husband, he would also always be a reminder of the days she'd lived in fear for her son.

His thoughts went in a new direction as he played and replayed time spent with Ed Maylor. Had he seen a flash of hatred in his deputy's eyes at any time? Had he sensed a dislike radiating from Maylor each time he'd given the man a command? He didn't know. He'd lost all objectivity.

"You okay?" It was Kessler who spoke, pulling Lucas from his thoughts.

"Yeah, I just want to find her," Lucas replied. He

grimaced, then added, "Even if it's just to give her a decent burial."

Those were the last words spoken for the next half hour. The sunshine overhead disappeared as trees choked off the light, casting them in a weird kind of twilight.

They began to check out the shanties they saw, abandoned structures, some of which had once held Cajun and Creole families with their colorful heritage.

In most cases it was evident just by looking that the shanties couldn't hold anyone captive. Roofs had tumbled, walls had rotted and there was little left except a broken-down frame.

Others needed to be checked thoroughly. Lucas and Kessler got out of the boat, guns drawn, to check the interiors of each structure, and each time they came up empty.

By six o'clock Lucas had lost hope. If they were going to make it back by dark they needed to start heading back. Maybe he'd been wrong. Maybe he'd been so desperate he'd only imagined the similarities between Maylor's voice and the tapes. After all, "I reckon," was a fairly common term.

Maybe the kidnapper was right. Maybe he wasn't a good choice for sheriff. Perhaps he did lack the investigative skills that made a good law-enforcement official.

Through the thick brush he spied another shanty and pointed to it. "We'll check this one out, then I guess we'd better head back. I don't want to be like any of those fishermen who got lost in Black Bay."

Remy guided the boat to the end of the rickety dock, and Lucas and Kessler jumped out. Another dead end, Lucas thought as they approached the structure, which looked as if a stiff wind might blow it into the water. Still he pulled his gun and approached.

Although the sound of the boat approaching would have been audible to anyone inside, Lucas and Kessler approached the structure silently, stealthily.

Lucas smelled the new-wood scent before they'd reached the front door. It was a scent that didn't belong, and a burst of adrenaline rocked through him.

There was only one way in…the closed door just ahead. For a moment he was afraid to go in, afraid that inside was the lifeless body of his sister.

Lucas swept through the door and stopped in surprise. A solid new wooden wall was just in front of him. There was a door with a small slat and a huge padlock.

"I'd say we've come to the right place," Kessler whispered from beside him.

The silence was deafening. Not a noise indicated any kind of life except the breathing of Lucas and Kessler. The silence scared him more than anything.

He drew a deep, unsteady breath and moved to the door. "Jenny?" He called her name, but there was no reply and a dull grief resounded inside him. He banged on the door. "Jenny? Jenny, are you in there?"

"Lucas?"

The faint reply dislodged a sob from his chest. "Jenny, honey, we're here. We're going to get you out of there. We're going to take you home."

Kessler looked around the area to try to find something to pry off the lock, but Lucas didn't want to wait. "Jenny, get away from the door. I'm going to shoot off the lock." He waited only a moment, then fired sideways at the lock, blowing it off the door.

He pushed through the now-unlocked door, and Jenny fell into his arms. "Jenny, honey, it's all right. You're safe now." She cried into the front of his shirt, clinging to him as if afraid he might disappear if she released him. And he cried, unable to stanch the tears that burned his eyes as he held his beloved sister in his arms.

"When I heard the boat I thought he was coming back, and when I heard your voice I thought it was a dream," she cried.

She raised her face to gaze up at him and for the first time he got a look at her swollen, black eye. Lucas's rage knew no boundaries. "I'll kill him," he said through clenched teeth. "Come on, let's get you out of here."

Within minutes they were back in the boat and headed in. As they rode, Jenny told them everything that had happened during her time in captivity. She told them of her greatest fear, that Billy would die in that shanty and there was nothing she could do about it. The only thing she could not tell them was who had held her there.

But Lucas knew. He *knew* it was Ed Maylor, and as he held his sister close, he swore that Maylor would spend the rest of his life behind bars.

Just before they reached the shore, Lucas called the office. Louis answered the phone. "Louis, we got her," he said. "We found Jenny and she's okay."

"Praise the Lord," Louis replied.

"You know where Maylor is?" Lucas asked.

"Yeah, I just sent him over to Mariah's place to spell Ben. Is there a problem?"

Lucas didn't reply. He couldn't speak around the lump of horror that filled his chest.

Chapter Fourteen

All day long Mariah had waited for news about Jenny, but none had been forthcoming. As dusk fell, she sent Billy in for a bath, then she sat at the kitchen table, surprised to find herself lonely.

She was beyond thrilled that her son was home where he belonged. The day had been filled with phone calls from well-wishers who had heard the news of his return. She and Billy had played games, baked a batch of cookies and watched movies, just enjoying being in each other's company.

Every time she looked at his little face, she kissed it, until finally he complained that she was kissing him way too much. "I'm trying to make up for all the days I didn't get to kiss you," she'd explained.

It was the usual routine for Billy to take a bath at this time in the evening, but never had Mariah experienced the kind of loneliness she felt at this moment. And she knew exactly what it was from.

She'd gotten used to Lucas's company. She hadn't realized how he'd filled up the house. He'd become a part of her everyday life, and she was surprised by the hole his absence had left behind.

It was crazy to miss him. She knew that the relationship they'd built had come into being in an alternate universe that had nothing to do with reality. It had been raw and intense, filled with enormous emotions.

Still, it had made her realize one thing—she was a young woman who didn't want to spend the rest of her life alone. Sure, Billy filled her life the way an eight-year-old could, but Lucas had awakened a hunger in her for something more, something adult and precious.

She wanted somebody to share her thoughts, somebody who would warm her through a cold, wintry night. She wanted conversation in the middle of the night, a secret smile over morning coffee.

When she'd arrived in Conja Creek, she'd been determined to keep all men at a distance, determined to build her world without any man in it in a meaningful way. Her need to be alone had been a selfish one, built on broken dreams and the pain of her failed marriage and the utter betrayal she'd suffered at Frank's hands.

But now she realized not only did she want a special man in her life, Billy also would thrive with a father figure in his. He deserved a man he could look up to, a man who would play catch with him and talk sports, as well as be a strong, masculine emotional support.

The problem was that, as she sat and tried to think about all the men she had met since coming to Conja Creek, her thoughts kept returning to Lucas.

Billy came into the kitchen clad in his navy-blue-and-yellow pajamas and smelling of soap and toothpaste. "Come here and give me a hug," she said to him.

He moved to her side and wrapped his arms around her neck, allowing her to hold him for a sweet long minute. It wouldn't be too long before he'd think he was too big for mommy hugs. She intended to take advantage before that time happened.

All too quickly he moved out of her arms. "Can I have some cookies and milk before I go to bed?"

Although normally she might have said no and offered him something less sweet, tonight she couldn't deny him. "Okay, four cookies and a glass of milk," she agreed. As he scooted into a chair at the table, she got up, poured his milk and placed the glass and the plate of cookies in front of him.

He took a sip of his milk then sighed. "I wish Jenny was here. She loves these chocolate chip cookies."

"I know you miss her. I miss her, too. Hopefully Lucas will find her real soon."

Billy's face lit up. "Is he coming over again?" He didn't wait for her answer. "I like him. I know all about him. Jenny told me he took care of her when she was little and she said he was the best brother in the world. Am I ever going to have a brother or a sister?"

Mariah laughed at the unexpected question. "I don't know, we'll have to see what the future holds. So you like Lucas?"

Billy nodded and wiped at his milk mustache. "I think maybe you should marry him and give me a little brother or sister."

Mariah's laughter was interrupted by the ring of the doorbell. "We'll talk about brother and sisters later. Finish your cookies," she said to Billy as she got up to answer. Maybe it was Lucas. Maybe he had news, or maybe he'd just come back again broken and grieving.

She opened the front door and was surprised to see

Deputy Ed Maylor standing on the porch. He offered her a friendly smile as she opened the screen door. "Deputy Maylor," she said.

"Hi, sorry to bother you, but I was wondering if I could trouble you for a glass of ice water. I've been sitting out front in my car and it's so hot. I forgot to pack water before I got here."

"Of course, please come in." She ushered him inside and through to the kitchen. "Billy, this is Deputy Maylor," she said to her son.

"Hi," Billy replied. "I'm a deputy, too. Lucas made me his official deputy."

"Oh, yeah, Saint Lucas," Maylor muttered under his breath. "Good with kids and nice to dogs."

Mariah looked at him sharply, unsure if she'd heard him right or not. Surely she had misunderstood. She got a glass from the cabinet, added ice, then filled it with water and placed it on the table in front of the deputy.

"Thanks," he said, then downed half the glass in three large swallows. "Mind if I have a little more?" She once again took the glass and moved back to the sink.

"You and Lucas, you got pretty close while your boy here was gone," Maylor said.

Something felt wrong, both in the question and with the man. A chill of unease walked up Mariah's spine. "Yeah, everybody loves Lucas Jamison," he continued. "The golden boy of Conja Creek. You know his parents were filthy rich, left him with enough money that he'd never have to work a day in his life. Not everybody is as lucky as our good sheriff."

Alarm bells screamed in Mariah's head. "Billy,

would you run to my bedroom and get my blue sweater out of my dresser drawer? I'm a little chilly."

There was no blue sweater in her dresser. She just wanted Billy away from this man, whose eyes flashed with something dark, something twisted. The flash was only there a moment, then gone. But she knew she hadn't just imagined it.

"Poor Lucas," he said. "I reckon he's going to be broken if he can't find his sister. I imagine he'll be too broken to stay here in Conja Creek."

"We still hope he will find her. Would you excuse me for just a moment? Billy must be having trouble finding my sweater." She didn't want for his response, but moved quickly down the hallway into the master bedroom.

Danger.

Danger. The word screamed through her senses. She could smell it in the air, feel it crawling icy fingers up her back, heard it shouting in her brain.

"Mom, I can't find..." Billy began.

"Shh," she told him. She quietly closed the bedroom door and locked it. "Help me move some furniture in front of this door," she said as she moved a chair and propped it beneath the door handle to create a barrier.

"Mom, what are you doing?" Billy asked in a whisper. He moved to the opposite side of the small wooden vanity and began to push as she pulled, wanting to get it in front of the door.

She was aware she might be overreacting, but she was functioning on a gut instinct that couldn't be ignored and that instinct screamed to her that she and Billy were in imminent danger.

"Mariah!" Maylor's heavy fist banged on the door.

The doorknob rattled and Mariah's heart boomed in her chest. "Hey, what are you doing in there? Come on out. I need to talk to you."

Mariah pointed Billy into the bathroom. "Go, close the door and lock it," she instructed. "Don't open it unless I tell you to. No matter what you hear, don't come out of there."

Thankfully he didn't hesitate but instantly obeyed as if he sensed the danger, too. She raced to the phone on the nightstand and picked it up. Dead. Oh God, help them. And her cell phone was in her purse on the kitchen counter.

Maylor banged again on the door, then laughed. "You really think a flimsy little lock is going to keep me out? Open the damn door."

"Just go away. I don't want to talk to you," she cried.

"Well, I want to talk to you. Now open the door." His voice had changed, deepened to a guttural growl.

"Why are you doing this?" she screamed.

"Because I hate him." A fist fell again, vibrating the door on its hinges. "He needs to suffer. I'm going to make him suffer." That voice, a low growl of rage, torched her fear even hotter. She knew that voice. It was the voice of the man who had taken her son, the man who had left messages on her answering machine.

Frantically Mariah looked around for a weapon she could use if he managed to get through the door. "Ed, be reasonable," she said as she searched the room. "You let Billy go. Nobody has been hurt yet. You can get help and everything will be all right." There had to be some humanity left in the man, he'd released Billy when Billy had been so sick.

"That was a mistake," Ed yelled through the door. "I should have left him there. I was weak, but I'm not weak now." Once again he hit the door and it splintered from the frame.

Mariah screamed, knowing that within seconds he'd be in the room. She picked up a heavy candlestick, but in her heart she knew it would do her little good. Deputy Maylor was armed with a gun.

He slammed into the door once again, and more splintering occurred. Mariah braced herself in front of the bathroom door, knowing he'd have to kill her in order to get past her to her son.

She screamed again, as loud as she could, hoping that her cries might alert a neighbor, a passerby, anyone who would come to help.

The door exploded inward and Maylor easily shoved the chair and the vanity aside and stepped into the room. He laughed as he saw her wielding the candlestick. "What are you going to do with that?" He pulled his gun and pointed it at her.

Tears blurred Mariah's vision. "Why do you want to hurt us? Billy and I have never done anything to you."

"Because he cares about you!" The cords in Maylor's neck stuck out as he screamed at her. "And I need to destroy everything he has, everything that's important to him."

"But why?" She needed an answer that made sense, a reason why all of this was happening.

"Maylor." The voice came from the hallway. Lucas's voice, strong and sure and filled with a simmering rage. "It's over. Throw your gun down and back away from her."

Maylor whirled around to face Lucas. "Ah, there he is, the golden boy of Conja Creek, the man born with a silver spoon in his mouth." The hatred dripped from Maylor's voice.

"I said it's over," Lucas said.

Mariah started to move, but Maylor glanced over and swung his gun at her. "Stay where you are," he demanded. "Both of you stay where you are." He swung the gun back in Lucas's direction.

"You think you're better than everyone else, living in that fancy mansion of yours, treating the rest of us like we're nothing but your servants." His voice was a hiss of hatred.

"I'm warning you, Maylor, toss your gun down. I don't want to hurt you, but I will if I have to," Lucas replied. "Throw down your gun and we can talk about this."

"There's nothing to talk about, there's nothing more to say." Spittle flew from Maylor as he screamed the words, obviously out of control as he waved the gun first in Mariah's direction, then at Lucas. "I'm better than your errand boy. Fetch me a burger, Maylor. Pick me up some clothes, Maylor. I crawled out of that swamp to make something of myself, but it's people like you who keep us down."

Mariah's heart thundered as Maylor appeared to spin completely out of control. As she saw him turn to face her once again, his gun hand rising, she screamed and closed her eyes and at the same time the sound of a shot boomed through the air.

She opened her eyes to see Maylor sprawled on the ground. He clutched his bloody shoulder and writhed in pain. Lucas entered the bedroom and kicked Maylor's gun across the room. "It's over," he said once again as Agent Kessler appeared at his side. "And you're lucky there's an FBI agent here to keep me from beating you to death."

Maylor winced, but forced a grotesque grin to his face. "I still win," he said softly. "You'll never find your sister. You'll never see Jenny again."

"Wrong," Lucas replied. "Jenny is right now at the Conja Creek Memorial Hospital. We found her in the place where you were raised, that little shanty in Black Bay. You're the loser in this little game of yours, Maylor."

Lucas reached down and jerked the deputy to his feet, unmindful of Maylor's yelp of pain. "Agent Kessler, would you please take this piece of garbage out?"

"It would be a pleasure," Kessler replied.

The moment they left the room Mariah raced to the bathroom and knocked on the door. "Billy, it's okay now. You can come out."

The bathroom door opened and Billy launched himself into his mother's arms. Mariah hugged him until he protested that she was squeezing the life out of him. Then Lucas hugged them both. Mariah hid her face in his chest, her arms around the two men in her life.

"It's okay now," Lucas said, calming both of them. "It's all over now."

When he released them, Billy looked up at him with tear-filled eyes. "Even though I'm an official deputy, I was scared."

Lucas crouched next to him. "And even though I'm an official sheriff, I was scared, too. But he won't bother us anymore. He's going to go to prison for a very long time."

"Is it true?" Mariah asked. "Is it true that you found Jenny?"

He nodded. "I was listening to the kidnapper tapes and suddenly I realized what was so familiar about that voice. I suspected it was Ed's. I found out that he'd been raised in the swamp, in a shanty in Black Bay, so with Remy Troulous as a guide we went hunting and we found her. I called the office as soon as we hit land, and Louis told me he'd just dispatched Maylor to come over here and sit on you and Billy. Remy and Wally took Jenny to the hospital and I came here." His eyes darkened. "Thank God I got here when I did."

"Is Jenny all right?" Billy asked. "Can we go see her?" He looked at Mariah who in turn looked at Lucas.

"I imagine she'll be in the hospital until at least sometime tomorrow."

Mariah smiled at her son. "We'll go see her in the morning. Tonight I'm sure what she needs more than anything is some time with her brother and some sleep."

"I'll need a report of everything that happened here," Lucas said.

"It can wait until tomorrow." She placed a hand on his arm. "Go see your sister, Lucas. I'm sure that's all she needs right now."

"You'll be safe now. It's really over." He pulled her to him for a quick embrace, then turned and left.

Mariah watched him go and she had a feeling of something important ending that she wished she could hang on to but feared she'd never experience again.

JENNY WAS LYING on her side facing away from the door when Lucas stepped quietly into her room. He'd already spoken to the doctor, who had assured him that other than the blackened eye, Jenny seemed to be fine. They were keeping her overnight for observation, and he expected she'd be released the next day.

A call to Kessler had let Lucas know that Maylor was someplace in the hospital, under guard and being treated for the gunshot wound to his shoulder. Kessler had assured him that once Maylor was fit to leave the hospital, he'd be whisked right into a jail cell.

Lucas approached Jenny's bed softly, his heart filled with an overwhelming whirl of mixed emotions. Love, relief and guilt all mixed inside him and he fought back tears.

"Jenny." He spoke her name softly.

She turned to face him and the shock of her black, swollen eye made him want to weep. "Lucas," she replied with a huge smile that warmed him to his toes. She reached out a hand. "Did you catch the bad guy?"

He nodded and took her hand in his, noticing the cracked and broken nails from where she had tried to pry off the boards in an effort to escape. "It was Ed Maylor."

"*Deputy* Maylor?"

"Yeah, but he's not going to hurt anyone ever again."

"And Billy and Mariah?" Worry deepened the blue of her eyes.

"Are fine," he assured her. The knot of emotion grew thicker, tighter in his chest. "God, Jenny, I thought I'd lost you."

"I'm sorry, Lucas." Tears filled her eyes. "I'm sorry about all this. I must have done something stupid for this to have happened."

"No, don't say that. This wasn't about you, Jenny. It had nothing to do with anything you did. And you aren't stupid. You're smart and funny and if you want to be a teacher that's okay with me. If you want to wear that red dress that I think is way too short, that's okay, too. Your life is yours to live, and I'll support you whatever you decide to do."

She uttered a small laugh through her tears. "Jeez, I should get kidnapped more often."

Lucas released her hand and grabbed a chair so he could sit by the side of her bed. There were so many things he wanted to tell her, so many things he needed to say. "Jenny, over the last couple of days I've had a lot of time to think, and I'm sorry for being too much of a big brother and not enough of a friend."

She rolled over on her side to face him. "Sometimes I don't know how you put up with me," she exclaimed, tears once again filling her eyes. "You should hate me."

He looked at her in surprise. "Hate you for what?"

"For ruining your marriage, for ruining your life," she cried.

"Oh, Jenny," he said softly. He hadn't realized the kind of baggage she'd been carrying for far too long. "You didn't ruin anything for me. You've been the best part of my life. As far as my marriage is concerned, all you did was save me a couple of miserable years and a messy divorce down the line." He took her hand in his again.

"I've been so afraid that somehow, someway you might turn out like Mom, I haven't paid enough attention to what a great woman you've become. Billy said you made him not be afraid. It was because of you that he was released." He reached over and touched the side of her face with the blackened eye. "You're my hero, Jenny. You make me so proud and from now on I'm backing off. You choose your path through life and I know you'll be just fine."

As he saw the love in Jenny's eyes, love coupled with pride, he knew they were going to be okay. She was going to be all right.

They talked for hours, deep into the night. They spoke about their mother, who had been emotionally unavailable to them both. He talked about his fear for her and his need to be both father and mother, a need that had made him too strong, too severe.

Their talk was filled with tears and laughter and healing for both of them. He stayed at her bedside long after she'd drifted to sleep, his mind racing with everything that had happened.

It was almost two in the morning when Agent Kessler motioned to him from the hallway. Lucas rose and joined him.

"How's she doing?" Kessler asked.

"She's going to be just fine," Lucas replied. "How's Maylor?"

"It was just a flesh wound. The doctor stitched him up, and he's already back at the jail. He's crazy, Lucas. For some reason he honed in on you with all his hatred and it pushed him over the edge."

"I just can't believe I didn't see it," Lucas replied. "I worked with him every day and I didn't see it. I keep thinking I missed something that I should have seen."

"You saw it when it counted the most." Kessler released a tired sigh. "I just have some paperwork to take care of, then I'll be out of here. I wanted to tell you that it was a pleasure to work with you and the rest of your men."

"And I appreciate all your help," Lucas replied. The two men shook hands.

Kessler smiled at him. "You're a good sheriff, Lucas. And the loyalty of your men speaks highly of the kind of boss you are. Don't let the ravings of a lunatic make you second-guess yourself." Kessler clapped him on the back then walked away.

As Lucas watched him go, he realized it was all truly over. Billy and Jenny were home safe, the bad guy was in jail and it was time to get back to something resembling a normal life.

He should be feeling euphoric. He should be feeling an immense sense of satisfaction. But any satisfaction he felt was tinged with a faint feeling of sadness. It was over, and that meant it was time for him to let go of Mariah.

She deserved a happy life with her son, a life without a reminder of everything they had been through. He'd held on to Jenny for too long, long after it was time to let go. He cared too much about Mariah to make the same mistake. He had to let her go.

MARIAH WAS VAGUELY disappointed when she and Billy arrived at the hospital to see Jenny, and Lucas wasn't there. She told herself it was for the best, but she'd hoped to see him there with a smile on his face and his eyes no longer burdened with the darkness of despair.

Even though she knew the relationship they'd shared had been forged by mutual fear, shared grief and dire circumstances, she couldn't help that her heart somehow had gotten involved.

"Your eye looks awesome," Billy said to Jenny. He leaned over her hospital bed to get a closer look. "It's kinda turning green."

Jenny laughed. "Only an eight-year-old boy would think a black eye was awesome."

"When are you coming home?" Billy asked. "Mom bought me a new game and I want to play it with you."

"The doctor said I can get out of here as soon as the paperwork is all done," Jenny replied.

"You want us to hang around and drive you home?" Mariah asked.

"Lucas is supposed to be coming to get me. He should be here soon. I don't know exactly what happened in the time that I was gone, but I have a feeling some alien replaced my brother with a pod person," Jenny said.

"What do you mean?" Mariah asked.

"Lucas and I had a long talk last night and he told me he was going to back off, let me make my own choices and be as supportive as he could be. I think things are going to be different between us, different in a good way."

"I'm glad," Mariah said. So, Lucas had taken her words to heart. She was glad for the joy that shone from Jenny's eyes.

Minutes later, as she and Billy drove home, she wondered if maybe somehow that had been her job through this whole ordeal, to give Lucas the strength to let go of his sister, to help them reach an adult relationship. If that were the case, then she'd obviously accomplished her job. So, why did she feel so bereft?

As soon as they got home Billy set up the kitchen

table with his new game in anticipation of Jenny's homecoming, then he went into his room to make a banner that read Welcome Home.

Mariah sat at the table and thought of all the hours she'd shared this space with Lucas. She'd spent years married to Frank, but in the space of a week she'd shared more of herself and learned more about Lucas than she ever had with Frank in her years of marriage.

A half hour later Jenny arrived with Lucas. Billy answered the door and ushered them inside. Mariah tried to slow the quickening beat of her heart as Lucas came into the kitchen.

He filled the space with his presence and that sweet familiar scent of his. He flashed her a smile that appeared slightly strained, and that more than anything else let her know that whatever they had shared had been just a moment in time and nothing else.

"Oh, it's so nice to be back," Jenny exclaimed.

"You want to play a game now?" Billy said eagerly.

"Why don't you two play a game while I have a talk with Mariah," Lucas said.

Loose ends, she thought a moment later as she allowed him to lead her to the front porch. He probably needed to finish up a report of some sort.

They stepped into the bright sunshine, and Mariah looked up at him curiously. He released a deep sigh, then ran his hand through his hair in a gesture she'd seen a hundred times before in the past couple of days.

He stepped to the edge of the porch and looked at the neighborhood, not speaking for several minutes. Tension built between them and Mariah wondered what was going through his head.

She walked up behind him and touched his back. "Lucas? Is something wrong?"

He spun around to face her, and for the first time she couldn't read his emotions, couldn't guess at his thoughts. "We did this all backward, Mariah. I took you to bed before I ever got a chance to take you to dinner. We built this crazy relationship and I don't know about you, but now that everything is over, I can't seem to get rid of the feelings I have for you and I don't know what to do about them."

A swell of emotion filled her chest. She was in love with this man. It didn't matter that the love had come at a time of intense drama. It didn't matter that it had bloomed in the space of only a handful of days.

"I'd think the first thing you should do about them is ask me out to dinner," she replied.

His face lost some of its tension and his eyes lightened. "And you'd go out with me?"

"I would, because those feelings you talk about having for me, I have them for you, too." Her heart had started beating so fast it threatened to beat right out of her chest.

He took three steps to stand directly in front of her, and there was no denying the glimmer of desire that shone from his eyes. "I don't want to be a reminder of the bad time you've just experienced," he said. "If you need me to stay away in order for you to put this all behind you, I'll understand."

She moved closer to him, breathing in the scent of him that smelled like home. "Lucas, you aren't a reminder of everything bad that's happened over the past week. You're my reminder of everything good.

When I was scared, it was your arms that held me. When I was filled with despair, it was your voice that soothed me. And when I thought I was dead inside, you brought me back to life. I'm in love with you, Lucas, and if you don't take me in your arms right now and kiss me I don't know what I'll do."

He didn't hesitate. He wrapped her up in his arms and took her lips with his. The kiss was soft and sweet but with a simmering heat that promised a lifetime of desire.

Reluctantly he pulled his mouth from hers and kissed the skin just beneath her ear. "If we keep this up, we'll never have a dinner out," he whispered.

She gave a shaky laugh and stepped out of his embrace. "At the moment, eating is the last thing on my mind."

His gaze held hers and he sobered. "I can't promise you that all of our time together will be as exciting as what we've already shared."

"Thank goodness for that," she replied, then laughed.

"What?" he asked.

"Poor Richard," she said.

Lucas frowned. "What about him?"

She moved back into his arms, loving the way she fit so perfectly against him, the way his eyes flared hotly at her nearness. "I don't think Richard is going to enjoy the fact that his secretary and his sheriff are an item."

He smiled at her and in his eyes she saw her future. "Then he doesn't have to dance at our wedding," he murmured just before he kissed her again.

Epilogue

"It was a beautiful ceremony," Mariah said as she and Lucas walked toward the white tent where punch and cake were being served.

Nearby, the bride and groom were receiving the best wishes of friends and family. Amanda Rockport made a lovely bride, and the look she exchanged with her new husband, Sawyer, spoke of the love that had brought them together. She'd come into his home as a nanny for Sawyer's daughter and now found herself a bride.

Lucas tugged at his tie. "Yeah, it was nice." He dropped his hand to her back and gently led her toward the table where the punch was located. "Sawyer looks happy, and that's what's important to me. After his last marriage he deserves all the good that comes to him and Amanda."

"And Melanie," Mariah reminded him. She glanced over to where Sawyer's daughter and Mariah's son sat on a nearby bench eating cake.

She and Lucas got their punch, then sat in two of the white chairs that had been provided for the occasion. As she sipped from her cup and looked around, she thought of how quickly the past month had passed by.

There had been a lot of changes. Jenny had moved into her own little apartment. She'd enrolled in college for the fall semester and was looking forward to getting her teaching degree. She wasn't dating anyone, telling Mariah that she wanted to find out what kind of person she was on her own before she added someone else into the mix.

Ed Maylor had pleaded guilty to the charge of kidnapping, saving the taxpayers the expenses of a full-fledged trial. For his own safety he'd been sentenced to spending his time in a prison where hopefully none of the other inmates would know that he was once supposed to be one of the good guys.

Frank had been arrested for domestic violence against his newest girlfriend and was spending the next eight months in jail. Mariah didn't expect to ever hear from him again.

"Well, well, if it isn't the most gossiped-about couple in Conja Creek," Jackson Burdeaux exclaimed as he joined them.

Mariah smiled at the handsome criminal defense attorney. "Hi, Jackson." Several times over the past couple of weeks he'd stopped by to spend a little time with the boy he'd picked up on the side of the road. Billy had taken to calling him Uncle Jackson, and Jackson seemed pleased by the honor.

He sat next to Lucas. "When are you two going to do the wedding thing?" he asked. "Your deputies are taking bets, you know. Half are betting you won't be a single man by Christmas and the other half are betting you won't be single by the end of the month."

Lucas laughed. "We haven't set a date yet." He

looked at Mariah, and as always her heart quickened its pace at the warmth and love that was in his gaze.

Their growing love for each other was the most amazing thing the past month had brought. Each of them had feared that what they'd gone through with the kidnapping had somehow manufactured a false emotion. But in the weeks since, they'd both been assured that what they felt was real and lasting.

"Nice that things have calmed down," Jackson observed and looked at Lucas. "Must be great to just be dealing with the usual crimes and misdemeanors for a change."

"Conja Creek has seen enough murder and mayhem," Lucas agreed. "Between the Bennett case and then Maylor, I'd say we're due for a little quiet time."

Jackson drained his punch cup and stood. "Enjoy it while you can, because there's one thing I've learned as a criminal defense attorney. As long as you have people, you have people who do bad things to each other."

Lucas laughed. "I'll say one thing for you, Jackson. You sure know how to put a damper on a party," he said dryly.

Jackson cast them a sheepish grin. "Sorry about that. I have a bad feeling in my gut, like we're all just holding our breaths until the next shoe falls." He winked at Mariah. "I think I'll feel better if I go chat up that pretty bridesmaid. I heard she's single."

"Go show her some of that Jackson charm," Lucas said to his friend. "Before the party is over she'll be putty in your hands."

Mariah watched as Jackson walked toward the bridesmaid in the reception line, then turned to smile at Lucas. "I would guess that Jackson was the heart-breaker in your group of friends."

"You'd guess right," Lucas replied. "I have a feeling when Jackson falls, he's going to fall hard."

"Speaking of falling hard..." She took his hand in hers. "I've fallen hard for you, Sheriff Jamison."

"And best of all I've fallen just as hard for you," he replied. "How about we blow this place and go back to your house. We'll order in some pizza, play some games with Billy and then when he goes to bed we'll play some different kind of games."

"Why, Sheriff, that's the best idea I've heard all day." Mariah's heart swelled as moments later they walked to Lucas's car. Billy rode piggyback on Lucas, his boyish laughter filling the air.

Over the past month a wonderful relationship had grown between the two most important men in her life. Billy adored Lucas, and the feeling was mutual and their relationship was both loving and healthy.

This was the family she'd always wanted, and she and Lucas had already agreed that another child was someplace in their future.

As she slid into the passenger seat, she smiled at Lucas, the secret, knowing smile of a woman who knew she loved and was loved.

* * * * *

Be sure to read Carla Cassidy's next
romantic and thrilling story,
NATURAL-BORN PROTECTOR.
Coming in September 2008
from Silhouette Romantic Suspense!

The Colton family is back!
Enjoy a sneak preview of
COLTON'S SECRET SERVICE by Marie Ferrarella,
part of THE COLTONS: FAMILY FIRST *miniseries.*

Available from Silhouette Romantic Suspense
in September 2008.

He cautioned himself to be leery. He was human and he'd been conned before. But never by anyone nearly so attractive. Never by anyone he'd felt so attracted to.

In her defense, Nick supposed that Georgie could actually be telling him the truth. That she was a victim in all this. He had his people back in California checking her out, to make sure she was who she said she was and had, as she claimed, not even been near a computer but on the road these last few months that the threats had been made.

In the meantime, he was doing his own checking out. Up close and exceedingly personal. So personal he could feel his blood stirring.

It had been a long time since he'd thought of himself as anything other than a law enforcement agent of one type or other. But Georgeann Grady made him remember that beneath the oaths he had taken and his devotion to duty, there beat the heart of a man.

A man who'd been far too long without the touch of a woman.

He watched as the light from the fireplace caressed the outline of Georgie's small, trim, jean-clad body as she moved about the rustic living room that could have easily come off the set of a Hollywood Western. Except that it was genuine.

As genuine as she claimed to be?

Something inside of him hoped so.

He wasn't supposed to be taking sides. His only interest in being here was to guarantee Senator Joe Colton's safety as the latter continued to make his bid for the presidency. Everything else was supposed to be secondary, but, Nick had to silently admit, that was just a wee bit hard to remember right now.

Earlier, before she'd put her precocious handful of a daughter to bed, Georgie had fed his appetite by whipping up some kind of a delicious concoction out of the vegetables she'd pulled from her garden. Vegetables that, by all rights, should have been withered and dried. She'd mentioned that a friend came by on occasion to weed and tend it. Still, it surprised him that somehow she'd managed to make something mouthwatering out of it.

Almost as mouthwatering as she looked to him right at this moment.

Again, he was reminded of the appetite that hadn't been fed, hadn't been satisfied.

And wasn't going to be, Nick sternly told himself. At least not now. Maybe later, when things took on a more definite shape and all the questions in his head were answered to his satisfaction, there would be time to explore this feeling. This woman. But not now.

Damn it.

"Sorry about the lack of light," Georgie said, breaking in to his train of thought as she turned around to face him. If she noticed the way he was looking at her, she gave no indication. "But I don't see a point in paying for electricity if I'm not going to be here. Besides, Emmie really enjoys camping out. She likes roughing it."

"And you?" Nick asked, moving closer to her, so close that a whisper would have trouble fitting in. "What do you like?"

The very breath stopped in Georgie's throat as she looked up at him.

"I think you've got a fair shot of guessing that one," she told him softly.

* * * * *

Be sure to look for COLTON'S SECRET SERVICE
and the other following titles from
THE COLTONS: FAMILY FIRST *miniseries:*
RANCHER'S REDEMPTION by Beth Cornelison
THE SHERIFF'S AMNESIAC BRIDE
by Linda Conrad
SOLDIER'S SECRET CHILD by Caridad Piñeiro
BABY'S WATCH by Justine Davis
A HERO OF HER OWN by Carla Cassidy

Silhouette®

Romantic
SUSPENSE

**Sparked by Danger,
Fueled by Passion.**

The Coltons Are Back!

Marie Ferrarella
Colton's Secret Service

The Coltons: Family First

On a mission to protect a senator, Secret Service agent
Nick Sheffield tracks down a threatening message only
to discover Georgie Gradie Colton, a rodeo-riding single
mom, who insists on her innocence. Nick is instantly
taken with the feisty redhead, but vows not to let his
feelings interfere with his mission. Now he must figure
out if this woman is conning him or if he can trust her
and the passion they share....

Available September wherever books are sold.

Look for upcoming Colton titles
from Silhouette Romantic Suspense:

RANCHER'S REDEMPTION by Beth Cornelison, Available October
THE SHERIFF'S AMNESIAC BRIDE by Linda Conrad, Available November
SOLDIER'S SECRET CHILD by Caridad Piñeiro, Available December
BABY'S WATCH by Justine Davis, Available January 2009
A HERO OF HER OWN by Carla Cassidy, Available February 2009

Visit Silhouette Books at www.eHarlequin.com   SRS27598

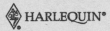

INTRIGUE

INTRIGUE'S
ULTIMATE
HEROES

★

6 HEROES. 6 STORIES.
ONE MONTH TO READ THEM ALL.

Harlequin Intrigue is dedicating
the month of September to those
heroes among men. Courageous
police, sexy spies, brave bodyguards—
they are all Intrigue's Ultimate Heroes.

In September, collect all 6.

REQUEST YOUR FREE BOOKS!

2 FREE NOVELS PLUS 2 FREE GIFTS!

Breathtaking Romantic Suspense

YES! Please send me 2 FREE Harlequin Intrigue® novels and my 2 FREE gifts (gifts are worth about $10). After receiving them, if I don't wish to receive any more books, I can return the shipping statement marked "cancel." If I don't cancel, I will receive 6 brand-new novels every month and be billed just $4.24 per book in the U.S. or $4.99 per book in Canada, plus 25¢ shipping and handling per book and applicable taxes, if any*. That's a savings of close to 15% off the cover price! I understand that accepting the 2 free books and gifts places me under no obligation to buy anything. I can always return a shipment and cancel at any time. Even if I never buy another book from Harlequin, the two free books and gifts are mine to keep forever.

182 HDN EEZ7   382 HDN EEZK

Name	(PLEASE PRINT)	
Address		Apt. #
City	State/Prov.	Zip/Postal Code

Signature (if under 18, a parent or guardian must sign)

Mail to the **Harlequin Reader Service:**
IN U.S.A.: P.O. Box 1867, Buffalo, NY 14240-1867
IN CANADA: P.O. Box 609, Fort Erie, Ontario L2A 5X3

Not valid to current subscribers of Harlequin Intrigue books.

Want to try two free books from another line?
Call 1-800-873-8635 or visit www.morefreebooks.com.

* Terms and prices subject to change without notice. N.Y. residents add applicable sales tax. Canadian residents will be charged applicable provincial taxes and GST. Offer not valid in Quebec. This offer is limited to one order per household. All orders subject to approval. Credit or debit balances in a customer's account(s) may be offset by any other outstanding balance owed by or to the customer. Please allow 4 to 6 weeks for delivery. Offer available while quantities last.

Your Privacy: Harlequin is committed to protecting your privacy. Our Privacy Policy is available online at www.eHarlequin.com or upon request from the Reader Service. From time to time we make our lists of customers available to reputable third parties who may have a product or service of interest to you. If you would prefer we not share your name and address, please check here. ☐

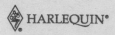

INTRIGUE

COMING NEXT MONTH

INTRIGUE'S
ULTIMATE
HEROES
★

#1083 MONTANA ROYALTY by B.J. Daniels
Whitehorse, Montana
Devlin Barrow wasn't like any cowboy Rory Buchanan had ever rode with. The European stud brought status to her ranch—as well as a trail of assassins and royal intrigue.

#1084 BODYGUARD TO THE BRIDE by Dani Sinclair
Xavier Drake had been on difficult missions before, but none more challenging than posing as Zoe Linden's bodyguard. Once he got his hands on the pregnant bride, it would be tough giving her away.

#1085 SHEIK PROTECTOR by Dana Marton
Karim Abdullah was the most honorable sheik and the fiercest warrior throughout the desert kingdom. On his word he vowed to protect Julia Gardner and her unborn child—the future prince of his war-torn land.

#1086 SOLVING THE MYSTERIOUS STRANGER
by Mallory Kane
The Curse of Raven's Cliff
The fortune told of a dark and mysterious stranger who had the power to save Raven's Cliff. But could Cole Robinson do it without sacrificing the town's favorite daughter, Amelia Hopkins?

#1087 SECRET AGENT, SECRET FATHER by Donna Young
Jacob Lomax awoke with no memory and an overpowering instinct for survival. In a race against time, the secret agent had to reconstruct the last twenty-four hours of his life, if he was to save Grace Renne and the unborn child that may be his.

#1088 COWBOY ALIBI by Paula Graves
Tough, embittered Wyoming police chief Joe Garrison had one goal: finding the person responsible for his brother's murder. But when a beautiful amnesiac Jane Doe surfaced in need of his help, his quest for justice turned into the fight of their lives.